What happe
become love
find out…

'You ought to co........ ...... warning for
young men!'

'It never bothered you,' said Bella, more
sharply than she had intended, and Josh pulled
away slightly, to look at her with a puzzled
frown.

'It was different for me.'

'I know,' she said.

Why? she wondered. Why didn't he desire her
like other men? He had never so much as
hinted that he wanted her as anything more
than a friend. And she would have been
appalled if he had, Bella reminded herself
honestly.

So why was it suddenly so hard to dance with
him like this?

Tender Romance™ is thrilled to present
the final book in this lively new trilogy from
JESSICA HART:

CITY BRIDES

*They're on the career ladder,
but just one step away from the altar!*

Meet Phoebe, Kate and Bella…

When their best friend gets married, these friends
suddenly realise that they're fast approaching thirty
and haven't yet found Mr Right—or even Mr Maybe!

Living together in the centre of London is a lot of fun,
but they refuse to admit that they spend more time
gossiping and groaning about the lack of eligible men
than actually looking for one…

But that's about to change.
If fate won't lend a hand, they'll make their own luck.
Whether it's a hired date or an engagement of
convenience, they're determined that the next
wedding invitation they see will be one of their own!

FIANCÉ WANTED FAST!
July (#3757)
THE BLIND-DATE PROPOSAL
August (#3761)
A WHIRLWIND ENGAGEMENT
September (#3765)

A WHIRLWIND ENGAGEMENT

BY
JESSICA HART

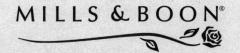

MILLS & BOON®

For Sally

DID YOU PURCHASE THIS BOOK WITHOUT A COVER?

If you did, you should be aware it is **stolen property** as it was reported *unsold and destroyed* by a retailer. Neither the author nor the publisher has received any payment for this book.

All the characters in this book have no existence outside the imagination of the author, and have no relation whatsoever to anyone bearing the same name or names. They are not even distantly inspired by any individual known or unknown to the author, and all the incidents are pure invention.

All Rights Reserved including the right of reproduction in whole or in part in any form. This edition is published by arrangement with Harlequin Enterprises II B.V. The text of this publication or any part thereof may not be reproduced or transmitted in any form or by any means, electronic or mechanical, including photocopying, recording, storage in an information retrieval system, or otherwise, without the written permission of the publisher.

This book is sold subject to the condition that it shall not, by way of trade or otherwise, be lent, resold, hired out or otherwise circulated without the prior consent of the publisher in any form of binding or cover other than that in which it is published and without a similar condition including this condition being imposed on the subsequent purchaser.

MILLS & BOON and MILLS & BOON with the Rose Device are registered trademarks of the publisher.

First published in Great Britain 2003
Harlequin Mills & Boon Limited,
Eton House, 18-24 Paradise Road, Richmond, Surrey TW9 1SR

© Jessica Hart 2003

ISBN 0 263 83396 8

Set in Times Roman 10½ on 12 pt.
02-0903-51642

Printed and bound in Spain
by Litografía Rosés, S.A., Barcelona

CHAPTER ONE

'THERE'S Bella.' Aisling nudged Josh, and he turned in the pew to see Bella and Phoebe hurrying down the aisle.

As befitted best friends of the bride, they had pulled out all the stops. Phoebe was dark and striking in an acid-yellow suit, while Bella had gone for a more romantic look in what Josh inexpertly assessed as a floaty pink number, with a spectacular hat that was clearly intended to knock all the others in the congregation into the shade.

Josh didn't pretend to know about such things, but even he could see that she had probably succeeded. Even Aisling's hat, which had made him raise his brows when he first saw it that morning, seemed tame in comparison. Typical Bella, he thought affectionately. She had always had the ability to turn heads, with or without a hat.

Phoebe waved as she spotted Josh and Aisling, and pointed Bella in their direction before heading up to have a word with her husband, Gib, who was best man and waiting with a very nervous Finn in the front pew.

Josh saw Bella register his presence, and an odd expression flitted over her face. It even seemed to him that she hesitated before sliding into the pew beside them, and his brows drew together slightly. Bella was his best friend, but she had been oddly distant recently.

'Sorry I can't kiss you,' she said, indicating the enormous brim of her hat. 'This isn't designed for close contact.'

'Yes, it is a bit awkward, isn't it?' Josh ducked underneath to kiss her cheek, anyway, and was sure he felt her tense at the touch of his lips.

He frowned as he drew back. 'Is everything OK?'

'Yes, of course,' said Bella, but he noticed that she didn't meet his eyes as she leant round him to greet Aisling. 'You know what weddings are like,' she went on, sitting back. 'There's always some last-minute panic when things get a bit tense.'

Just a fraught morning, then, thought Josh, telling himself that explained the unusual brittleness of her smile. 'How is Kate?'

'A bit jittery, but she'll be fine. She should be here any minute.'

On his other side, Aisling leant forward to talk across him. 'I'm surprised you're not Kate's bridesmaid, Bella,' she said. 'You are her best friend, after all.'

'So is Phoebe.' Bella's tone was cool. 'And Kate's not very tall. She'd look ridiculous with both of us towering over her.'

'Yes, but Phoebe's married.'

'So?'

'So as the only unmarried friend left, it would have been quite natural if Kate had chosen you as her bridesmaid,' Aisling tried to explain.

'Oh, I think I'm a bit old for that, don't you?' said Bella pleasantly enough, but sitting between the two women Josh could feel a distinct undercurrent of tension.

'I wouldn't have thought so,' said Aisling. 'You can't be much more than thirty-five, surely?'

Josh cleared his throat and shifted in the pew. Aisling was treading on dangerous ground. Bella was very sensitive about her age for some unfathomable reason.

Glancing sideways, he saw Bella's blue eyes narrow beneath the brim of her hat. 'Not quite,' she said thinly. 'As it happens, I'm only thirty-two.'

And she shot a glance at Josh which said more clearly than words ever could that he wasn't even to *think* about adding 'nearly thirty-three'.

'Really?' Aisling was tactlessly surprised. 'I always thought you'd be more Josh's age since you were students together.'

'No, Josh was a bit older than the rest of us when he started,' said Bella grittily, and Josh decided it was time to change the subject.

'Is Kate not having any bridesmaids then?' he asked hurriedly.

'Alex is going to have the starring role all to herself. Alex is Finn's daughter,' Bella added for Aisling's benefit. 'She's absolutely thrilled—more excited than Kate, I think! She couldn't stand still while we were helping Kate get ready.'

She smiled at the memory. 'It's much more appropriate for Kate to have her stepdaughter, and anyway, if I'd been bridesmaid I wouldn't have been able to wear this hat!'

'And that would have been a crime,' said Josh solemnly.

Bella adjusted the hat on her head, and sent him a speculative glance from beneath the brim. 'What do you think of it?' she asked him.

'It's…very…big,' was the most diplomatic thing he could come up with.

She laughed and for a moment it was the old Bella beside him, her face vivid and the bright blue eyes alight with laughter. It made Josh realise how much he had missed her recently.

Not that he hadn't seen her, but somehow she just hadn't been herself. Their friendship had always been such an easy one, but recently Bella had been strangely constrained. Something was wrong, and Josh didn't like it. She had lost her sparkle, and he missed it.

Of course, she might be having problems with Will but he had seen Bella through more romantic crises than he cared to remember, and it had never affected her relationship with *him* before.

Maybe it was different this time. Maybe Will was more important to her than all the others.

For some reason, Josh didn't like that thought very much. Will wasn't nearly good enough for Bella in his opinion.

'Where's Will?' he asked trying not to betray his dislike of the other man. 'I was expecting him to be keeping a pew for you.'

Bella had picked up the order of service and was studying the front, which was embossed simply with the names Kate and Finn, and the date, 6th September. 'Will?' she said a little too casually. 'He's in Hong Kong.'

'Hong Kong!' Josh scowled. 'What's he doing there?'

'He's got a meeting,' said Bella, opening the order of service to look at the hymns.

Josh snorted contemptuously. 'When did he arrange that?'

'It came up at the last minute.'

'Couldn't he have arranged to go next week? He must have known about Kate's wedding for ages.'

Bella kept her eyes on the order of service. 'Yes, but this was important,' she said, sounding reticent. 'There was some kind of crisis and he had to drop everything and go.'

'You're important, too,' said Josh angrily.

That was typical of Will! Swanking off to the other side of the world instead of supporting Bella. Josh had always thought him a prat of the first order, and this just confirmed it.

He couldn't understand why Bella always went for men like Will. They were too smooth by half, in Josh's opinion. Will was suave and handsome and drove a Porsche, but he didn't impress Josh. When the chips were down, Will wasn't a man you could rely on, and his attitude to Bella just proved it.

'It's not as if he's a brain surgeon,' he went on pugnaciously. 'He doesn't *do* anything. He just sits in some plush office in the City and plays around with money. What's important about that?'

'It's his career,' said Bella, tight-lipped. 'And he doesn't just "play around" with money. He deals with millions and millions of pounds, and when something goes wrong with that kind of money, it can affect the international money markets which affect economies around the world, which affect our jobs and our income and our quality of life. I think that's important,' she finished defiantly.

Josh wasn't ready to be convinced that Will had any useful contribution to make to society. 'If I thought the economic stability of the world rested on Will's ability to rush off to Hong Kong at the drop of a hat, I'd be really scared,' he said. 'As it is, I suspect that the global economy wouldn't so much as totter if he'd left it until Monday instead so that he could be with you today.'

Bella glared at him. 'Look, what's your problem? If I understand why Will can't be here, and Kate understands, and Finn understands, I don't see why *you* can't!'

'I just think he should be here to support you,' said Josh stubbornly.

'I don't need support! I'm at the wedding of one of my dearest friends, surrounded by people who know me. Why would I need supporting?'

'I think Josh is concerned that you might be feeling a bit left out,' Aisling put in unwisely. 'He's told me how close you were to Phoebe and Kate when you all shared that house, and now they've both married and are moving on. I can see it might be quite a vulnerable time for you,' she finished with a sympathetic look.

Bella shot her a glance of dislike. 'If you're trying to suggest that I'm jealous, you're quite wrong,' she said clearly. 'I couldn't be happier for Kate, and for Phoebe. They've both found the perfect man for them, but I don't feel at all *left out*, as you put it, because I happen to have found the perfect man for me too. Will and I are very happy together, so I don't feel the slightest bit vulnerable or in need of support, thank you very much!'

'You don't seem very happy, Bella,' said Josh.

'That might have something to do with fact that my best friend and his girlfriend are busy slagging off my boyfriend and making me feel that I need to be pitied in some way!' she snapped back. 'Would that make *you* happy?'

Josh opened his mouth, but before he could reply Phoebe was scrambling into the pew beside Bella. 'Here she comes!' she said, blowing a kiss in Josh's direction and moving Bella along with a shove of her hip as the organ struck up the 'Bridal March'.

Bella found herself pressed against Josh, and expressed her feelings with a vigorous shove of her own which sent him shuffling into Aisling, who ended up squeezed against a pillar.

Not very dignified behaviour for a wedding, perhaps, but it made Bella feel a whole lot better.

Turning, Bella watched Kate coming slowly up the aisle on her beaming father's arm, and her throat tightened. It was such a cliché to describe a bride as radiant, but it really was the perfect word for Kate that day. Everything about her seemed to shine, and the brown eyes fixed on the man waiting for her at the altar were luminous with love.

Bella followed Kate's gaze and looked at Finn, who had turned and was watching his bride walk towards him. The expression on his face made her want to cry.

Would anyone ever look at *her* with that kind of desire? Bella wondered. She tried to imagine herself in Kate's place, but somehow she couldn't picture the man who would be waiting for her.

It wasn't going to be Will, anyway, in spite of what she had told Josh and Aisling. Aisling! What a stupid name, thought Bella. Apparently it was supposed to be pronounced Ashling, but she always made a point of saying it just as it was spelt, just to annoy. There was just something about Aisling that rubbed her up the wrong way.

Guiltily aware that she should be thinking about the fact that Kate and Finn were getting married at last, Bella hurriedly fixed her eyes on the bride and groom.

Kate had turned and was giving her bouquet to Alex, who was bursting with pride at her important role. Her tongue stuck out with concentration as she stepped back with the precious flowers, but when Finn winked at his daughter, her face lit up with a dazzling smile that brought tears to Bella's eyes.

It was a traditional country wedding in the village church, and Bella found herself absurdly moved by the familiar ceremony. She and Phoebe were not the only ones who spent most of the service wiping their eyes, and when the earlier clouds dissolved letting Kate and Finn emerge from the rose-edged porch into brilliant sunshine, they looked so right together that Bella started to cry all over again.

'This is awful,' she wept to Phoebe. 'I haven't cried this much since *Terms of Endearment*!'

'I know,' Phoebe sniffed. 'They just look so *happy*!'

'What's wrong with you two?' demanded Josh. 'Weddings are supposed to be joyful occasions!'

'It's a woman thing,' Gib told him knowledgeably. 'Apparently snivelling like this means they're having a good time. They'll be all right when they get some champagne inside them!'

Aisling wasn't crying, Bella couldn't help noticing. No fear of *her* mascara running! Instead she clung to Josh's arm looking cool and pretty in a simple aquamarine shift with an annoyingly stylish hat. Bella had been so pleased with her own hat, but next to Aisling's she was suddenly convinced that it seemed over-the-top and ridiculous.

Everything about Aisling made her feel that way. Where Aisling was quietly confident, she was loud. Aisling was elegant, she was blowsy. Aisling knew how to put up a tent and abseil down a cliff, she was city girl incarnate.

Aisling was perfect for Josh, in fact, and she was just his friend.

Bella turned quickly away and pinned on a bright smile to watch the photographs being taken. Gib had organised it well, and after the inevitable family groups, they moved rapidly onto photos of friends with the bride and groom. There was one of them with Kate's original housemates, Caro and Phoebe and Bella, with Caro and Phoebe's husbands, of course.

And then there was Kate and Finn with their close friends and partners, which meant Phoebe and Gib, Josh and Aisling, and Bella.

Bella was very conscious of being on her own in both photos. It was a new experience for her. She had always been the one with a boyfriend, while Phoebe and Kate moaned about the lack of men, so it was ironic that she should be the odd one out now.

Not that Bella had any intention of giving Aisling the

satisfaction of thinking that it bothered her. She kept a smile fixed to her face, and laughed and chatted animatedly as the last photographs were taken and the entire party walked back through the village to where a marquee had been erected in the garden of Kate's parents.

She thought she was putting on a pretty good show of not having a care in the world, but it didn't seem to fool Josh. Sometimes he knew her too well, thought Bella with an inward sigh, wishing he would stop asking if something was wrong. She didn't want to tell him that she was feeling edgy and unsettled, because then he would ask why, and she didn't know why.

Only that wasn't *quite* true, was it? She did know.

It was something to do with the way Aisling's arrival on the scene had brought her up short. Something to do with looking across the table at that engagement dinner for Kate and realising that Josh was no longer the familiar, slightly geeky student she had known for so long.

For Bella, it had been like finding herself suddenly face to face with a stranger. There was nothing obvious about Josh. He had a quiet, ordinary face, ordinary blue-grey eyes, ordinary brown hair, she had always known that.

But she had never before noticed how he had thickened out and grown into his looks, or how the fourteen years they had known each other had given him a solid, reassuring presence and an air of calm competence that was impressive without being intimidating.

She had never noticed his mouth before or his hands or throat or that line of his jaw. Never noticed that he had a great body. He wasn't exceptionally tall but he was lean and compactly muscled, and he moved with an easy, loose-limbed stride.

And now that she *had* noticed, Bella couldn't stop noticing.

It made her uneasy. This was *Josh*. Her best friend, the
one who had seen her through endless romantic ups and
downs. She had cried on his shoulder and laughed and
talked and hugged him without a thought for more than
ten years now. He had seen her without her make-up, seen
her tired and cross and sick and hungover, and she had
taken him for granted. Being with Josh had been like being
with Kate or Phoebe, as comfortable as an old pair of
slippers.

But now, suddenly, she didn't feel comfortable with him
any more and she didn't understand why. She just wanted
to go back to the way things had been before.

Here he was now. Bella felt her nerves crisp as Josh
came up to her in the marquee, and she took a steadying
slug of champagne. He was the same old Josh he had always been. It was nonsense to think that anything had
changed between them.

'Are you OK?' he said, eyeing her with concern.

'Of course. Why?'

'You seem a bit tense, that's all. I wondered if you and
Will might be having problems.'

'I don't know why you're so determined that my relationship with Will is a disaster,' said Bella, annoyed with
him for hitting the nail so unerringly on the head. 'What
could be wrong? Will's fantastic. He's incredibly attractive, generous, clever, successful…'

And he *was*, she reminded herself with a kind of desperation. She had been mad about Will when she first met
him. Why couldn't she feel like that again?

'I'm just missing him while he's away,' she offered,
hoping that the explanation would stop Josh probing
any further. 'And the house feels very empty without
Kate now.'

'It must do.' To her relief, Josh allowed himself to be diverted. 'Are you going to stay there on your own?'

'I think so. I only pay a token rent as it is. Phoebe doesn't need the money—one of the many advantages of having a rich husband!—so I can afford to have the house to myself.'

'I'm surprised you don't move in with Will if he's as perfect as you say he is,' sniffed Josh. 'Doesn't he want to "commit"?' he added, hooking sarcastic inverted commas around the word.

'That's good coming from you!' said Bella, provoked out of her awkwardness. 'You've never committed to anyone!'

'I'm just waiting for the right woman,' he said loftily.

'No, you're not,' she said. 'You're scared to take a risk.'

Josh's jaw dropped. 'How can you *say* that, Bella?'

'Yes, yes, I know that you've taken convoys through war zones and rescued people off mountains in blizzards and all that stuff,' she said with a dismissive wave of her hand.

Before he set up his own company to provide executive training a couple of years ago Josh had provided logistical support for expeditions. Most of them were providing disaster relief but sometimes he would organise fund-raising expeditions for the aid agencies he dealt with. Bella had never been able to understand why someone would want to pay good money to be tired and cold and terrified for a month, but they had always proved very popular.

'I know you've been in loads of dangerous situations,' she went on, 'but those are physical risks. Have you ever taken any other kind of risk?'

'It was risky setting up my own company,' said Josh, sounding a bit huffy.

Bella was unimpressed. 'That was a financial risk. I'm talking about emotional risks.'

Josh hunched a shoulder. 'You have to approach all risks the same way. Look at the situation logically, not emotionally, and balance the likelihood of possible outcomes.'

When he went all logical on her like that, Bella always wondered how on earth they had come to be friends. Mentally, she raised her eyes to heaven.

'It just so happens that as far as relationships are concerned I've never been convinced that the risk was worth taking,' he was saying, 'but it's not a question of being *scared*.'

The scared thing had obviously rankled.

'We're not all like you,' he accused her, 'investing everything in a relationship five minutes after you've met a man. You'd think experience would have taught you to keep something back, but no! You're barely over one disastrous affair before you plunge into another one!'

'Better that than dithering around on the edge for ever, wondering if you might just have missed the chance of a perfect relationship,' Bella retorted.

'And that's what you've got with Will, is it?' Josh asked sceptically.

She lifted her chin defiantly. 'I think so, yes.'

'So why not live together?'

'Because we're both happy as we are. We've each got our own place to live and that means we can give each other some space. We all need that.'

Josh didn't bother to hide his disbelief. 'You? You're the most sociable person I know! I can't see you hankering after your own space.'

'Perhaps you don't know me as well as you think you do,' said Bella crossly. 'As a matter of fact, I'm looking forward to living on my own. I've been getting gradually used to it since Kate has been spending so much time with Finn and Alex, so it won't be that different now. I might go back to sharing eventually,' she conceded, 'but it wouldn't be the same. Where would I find someone I'd get on with as well as Phoebe and Kate?'

'What about Aisling?' said Josh casually.

Bella looked wary. What *about* Aisling?

'She's looking for somewhere to live at the moment,' he explained. 'And you'd be bound to get on. I'd have thought she'd be perfect for you.'

What planet was he living on? Bella stared at him in disbelief. He didn't really see her and Aisling as bosom buddies, did he? Didn't he know her at all?

'I'm not sure we've got that much in common,' she said carefully.

Josh looked surprised. 'Don't you? I think you're very alike. Aisling's in marketing and you're in PR—they're not that different as careers go, are they? And she's a bit of a social butterfly, too.'

'I thought she spent her whole time climbing mountains or knocking up rafts out of a couple of tin cans and a piece of string?' said Bella a little sourly.

'She's got a lot of expedition experience,' Josh agreed, 'but she's a good-time girl like you on the side as well.'

Oh, right. So Aisling swung both ways. She could hack her way through a rainforest *and* wear lipstick. Bully for her. Bella took another slurp of champagne.

'She's not quite such a princess as you, though,' Josh was adding with something less than his usual tact. 'She doesn't actually require somewhere to plug in her hair-dryer when she's camping!'

Bella eyed him with some hostility. Josh had once in-sisted on taking her camping in the Yorkshire Dales, and had been appalled when he discovered that not only had she taken a hair-dryer with her but she had actually used it. He had never let her forget it. Bella was quite sure that Aisling had heard that story and laughed prettily at the idea that anyone could be quite that much of a city girl.

'I'm not sure Tooting would be very convenient for Aisling,' she said. 'It's not exactly handy for your office, is it?'

'Aisling's been trekking across the Sahara,' Josh pointed out. 'I don't think she would find changing tubes a problem!'

Well, that put *her* in her place, thought Bella grumpily.

'Yes, well, I'll talk to Phoebe,' she said without enthusiasm. 'It's her house, so it's her decision really.'

'Great,' said Josh. 'I'm sure Phoebe won't mind.'

'Where is Aisling, anyway?' said Bella. She had to get to Phoebe before Josh did. There was no way she was going to share a house with Aisling.

Josh looked around the marquee, and pointed. 'Over there, talking to Finn's sister.'

As if she had heard him, Aisling looked over, and beckoned imperatively. In spite of being anxious to get rid of him so she could go and find Phoebe, Bella couldn't believe it when Josh just *went*. He ought to have more pride, she thought crossly.

Still, now was her chance to grab Phoebe.

'So you will say no, won't you?' she begged when she had dragged Phoebe away from Gib and poured the whole story into her ears.

'If you want,' said Phoebe, 'but I don't know what I'm going to say to Josh. I can't think of any reason to object to Aisling. She seems very nice.'

'I don't like her,' said Bella.

'Why not?'

'I just don't,' she said a little sulkily. 'There's a little too much of that bubbly Irish charm if you ask me. And I don't think she's right for Josh.'

Phoebe looked at her narrowly. 'Are you sure you're not just jealous?'

'Jealous? *Jealous*?' spluttered Bella, spilling most of the champagne in her outrage. 'Don't be ridiculous! I have *never* been jealous of Josh, you know that. I've always got on really well with all his girlfriends.'

'Mmnn, but then none of them were at all like you.'

'Nor is Aisling!'

'Yes, she is. I'm sure that's why you don't like her. You've only got to look at her!'

Bella turned to stare across the marquee to where Aisling was snuggling up to Josh. She obviously couldn't keep her hands off him. Josh would hate that, Bella thought disapprovingly. He was definitely a behind-closed-doors sort of man.

On the other hand, he wasn't exactly fighting Aisling off, was he?

She looked away. 'I'm nothing like Aisling,' she told Phoebe. 'She's got red hair, for a start!'

'OK, but change the colour of her hair and eyes, and what have you got? She's ridiculously pretty, has legs up to her armpits, and that glamorous look that is just *so* different from Josh's previous girlfriends. Admit it, Bella, she's practically a clone!'

Bella wasn't prepared to admit anything of the kind. 'What, apart from looking completely different and having completely different personalities? I'd say all Aisling and I had in common was our gender! Josh is always telling me how practical she is and how she likes doing hearty things like climbing and camping.'

Phoebe shrugged. 'Have it your own way.'

'Anyway,' Bella went on, a defensive edge to her voice, 'Josh and I agreed a long time ago that we would just be friends. There's no question of jealousy.'

'Didn't you *ever* find him attractive?' asked Phoebe curiously, and try as she might, Bella couldn't quite make herself meet her friend's eyes.

'He wasn't my type,' she said.

'Do you think you were ever his?'

Had she been? For the first time Bella found herself wondering.

'He never said, and anyway, he always seemed to have some outdoorsy girl who didn't fuss about her hair or wear make-up or mind getting up at six to go potholing or whatever it was they used to do at weekends. Josh and I used to make each other laugh, and we had a great time doing that. We didn't want to spoil it by sleeping together.'

'Besides,' she added honestly, 'he wasn't at all attractive then. He was a bit thin and nerdy.'

Phoebe glanced across the marquee. 'He's changed,' she said.

'Yes,' said Bella, following her gaze. Through the crowds, she could just glimpse Josh. The lean, compact figure was at once alien and utterly familiar.

He was talking to someone out of sight, but as she watched he threw back his head and laughed, and her stomach abruptly disappeared, as if she had stumbled unawares off the edge of an abyss. The sensation of falling was so intense that Bella had to close her eyes against a sickening wave of vertigo, and when she opened them again she felt dizzy and hollow inside.

'Yes,' she said again. 'He has.'

There was a silence. Frightened by the strength of her physical response, Bella drank her champagne shakily, and it was some time before she realised that Phoebe was watching her expectantly.

'What?' she demanded, and Phoebe held up her hands, one still clutching her champagne glass.

'I didn't say anything!'

That was the worst thing about friends who knew you really well. They didn't need to say anything for you to know exactly what they were thinking!

'I'm not jealous, all right?'

'All right,' said Phoebe equably. 'So what is the problem?'

'Who says there's a problem?'

Phoebe sighed. 'Come on, Bella, it's obvious! Is it Will?'

'No.... Yes...sort of,' Bella admitted with a sigh.

'What happened?'

'Nothing, that's just it.' Bella stared miserably down into her glass. 'It's just that I've been feeling...I don't know...*restless*, I suppose, for a while. We haven't had an argument or anything. It was Will who suggested that we give each other some space, and I think that's all I need. I mean, Will's fantastic, isn't he?' She hated the doubtful note in her voice.

'He certainly seems very nice,' said Phoebe noncommittally.

'And drop-dead gorgeous and intelligent and solvent and not screwed up... What more could I ask for? He would have come today if I'd asked him,' she went on with a sigh. 'I need my head examined to let him go off to Hong Kong! What's *wrong* with me?'

'There's nothing wrong with you. Will just isn't the right man for you, that's all.'

'But if someone like Will isn't the right man, who is?'

'I don't know,' said Phoebe, 'but *you* will when you find him.'

CHAPTER TWO

BELLA wished she had Phoebe's confidence. She was beginning to wonder if there was something wrong with her. It wasn't that she was particularly vain, but she knew she was pretty, and there was never any shortage of men wanting to go out with her. Somehow, though, it never came to anything. She fell headlong into love and just as quickly out of it.

She might never find that special man, Bella thought glumly as she helped herself to a canapé, and now she might not even have Josh to fall back on. They had once agreed that if they both reached forty without finding anyone they would marry each other.

Bella actually remembered laughing at the time. The truth was that it had never occurred to her then that Josh might marry someone else. He was so self-contained that it was hard to imagine him sharing his life with anyone. None of his girlfriends had ever moved in with him.

Looking for him now, her eyes found him instinctively in the crowded marquee. There he was, Aisling clinging as usual to his arm, and no matter how much she wanted to think that he looked irritated by her possessiveness, she just couldn't do it.

Bella drifted around the edge of the marquee to get a better view. That was better. Now she could see Josh quite clearly, talking to Gib. He was wearing a morning suit, and the crisp white shirt made his skin, weathered from so much time spent in the tropics, look even browner than usual.

He looked surprisingly good in formal clothes, she thought. Even now, dressed identically to most of the other men in the marquee, he had the tough, competent air of a man who should be hacking his way through a jungle or bumping along a dusty track in faded khakis, not sipping champagne and eating canapés in an English garden.

Bella's gaze rested on him. Really, it was amazing that it had taken her so many years to realise what a great body he had, lean and hard and tautly muscled in an intriguingly restrained way. If she had walked into the marquee as a stranger, she would definitely have clocked him.

His face wasn't that bad either. Not jaw-droppingly handsome like Will, of course, but still, there was nothing actually wrong with it. He had nice eyes, creased around the edges from too much squinting at the sun, and they held a lurking smile sometimes that might be really quite disturbing if you weren't used to it, the way she was.

Nice mouth too, Bella thought judiciously. Not the kind of mouth you noticed at first, maybe—it was too quiet and cool for that—but if you looked at it for too long, something about it made you squirm suddenly.

Like that. A strange feeling shuddered down Bella's spine, and she jerked her eyes away.

It felt all wrong to be thinking about Josh like this. He was her friend, the one person she could talk to about anything at all.

Except this.

Bella imagined herself strolling over and saying, 'Hey, Josh, I was just thinking what a great body you have and wondering what it would be like to kiss you,' and she winced, picturing already his appalled expression. She couldn't do that to Josh.

More to the point, she couldn't do it to herself! Honesty was one thing, humiliation quite another.

Gib's attention had been claimed by another guest and, as Bella watched, Josh tightened his arm around Aisling and gave her a quick private kiss. The pain that sliced through her at the sight was so unexpected that it took Bella's breath away, and the champagne spilt from her glass as she flinched instinctively.

Bella turned abruptly away. This wouldn't do! She was the life and soul of a party, not someone who mooned around on the edges feeling left out. It was time to circulate and exert some of that charm she was so famous for.

She succeeded so well that one of Kate's young brothers informed her owlishly at the end of the reception that he had been in love with her since he was fourteen, and asked her to marry him. Touched and amused, Bella let him down kindly but secretly she couldn't help feeling a bit better. She might be tottering on the verge of thirty-three and she wasn't a camping queen like Aisling, but *some* men wanted her, even if they were only twenty-one and had been imbibing freely of their father's champagne.

She seemed to have developed a sudden attraction for very young men. At the ceilidh in the marquee that evening Bella found herself the centre of a group of besotted boys. Their undisguised admiration was very flattering of course, but she wasn't entirely sure that it was a good sign. Did she really look old enough to be in the market for a toy boy? Bella wondered.

Still, it was nice to feel wanted for a change, and she glanced across the marquee to where Josh had Aisling entwined around him as usual.

Determined to show Josh, should he happen to look in her direction, that she was having a wonderful time, Bella let one of her admirers after another swing her eagerly on the dance floor. Her partners appeared deaf to the bellowed instructions of the member of the band who was desperately trying to tell everyone the moves to the Scottish dances, but what they lacked in skill, they more than made up for in enthusiasm. More than once Bella found herself being spun out of control so that she ended up cannoning breathlessly into other couples. Fortunately few of them seemed to have a clue what they were doing either.

Bella told herself she was having a fantastic time, and laughed as she shook back her hair over her shoulders.

From another set, Josh watched her dazzle the boy she was dancing with. He couldn't be more than sixteen and obviously could hardly believe his luck, Josh thought indulgently. He had seen how effortlessly Bella had cast her spell over every man she came across. Even Kate's famously grumpy great-uncle had not been immune to the old Stevenson charm.

It had been the same ever since he had met her. Josh remembered the first time he had seen her. She had walked into the seminar room, blonde, beautiful and impossibly glamorous amongst all the other scruffy students, and when she smiled and sat down next to him, he had gulped like the schoolboy she was dancing with now.

There had been a starry quality about Bella, even then, he thought. For the first few weeks, he had gawked at her from a distance. She was so clearly out of his league, that it never occurred to him that they could ever be friends, but when he did get to know her properly, he was bowled over by the charm that made him feel as if she had been waiting all this time just to meet him, plain Josh Kingston. He had been amazed to discover how friendly and natural she was, and how funny. She might look like a princess, but she had an infectiously dirty laugh.

Not that Josh ever tried to take advantage of the closeness that grew up between them. His role was as a friend, the one constant male in the dizzying ups and downs of her romantic life.

And Josh didn't mind, or he told himself he didn't, anyway. At least that way he saw Bella, and he kept on seeing her in a way the men she fell in and out of love with didn't. None of them ever lasted very long. Bella might look sophisticated, but beneath her glossy veneer beat the heart of a true romantic, determined not to settle for anyone less than Mr Perfect.

Maybe she had found him in Will. He seemed an unlikely Mr Perfect to Josh, but he had never understood Bella's taste in men. He had wondered if things had run their course with Will earlier, when she had seemed tense and unhappy, but there was no sign of that now.

Josh's mouth curled affectionately as he watched Bella dancing up and down the line in the other set, laughing that laugh of hers. She was being swung around and around between each couple, her hair shimmering as it flew around her vivid face and her skirt swirling around those spectacular legs.

'Josh!' Aisling hissed at him, and he started as he realised that he was supposed to be joining hands and going down the set with her, not watching what was going on elsewhere.

He didn't get a chance to dance with Bella herself until much later in the evening.

'I'm tired,' she said when he held out his hand to pull her onto the dance floor.

'Tired? You? Never!'

'I am,' she protested. 'I've been dancing all night.'

She fanned her hot face, unwilling to let him know reluctant she was to take his hand. 'Ask Aisling.'

'She's dancing with Gib.'

'Honestly, Josh, I'm exhausted,' Bella tried, but Josh was determined.

'This isn't going to require any energy,' he said as the band struck up a slow tune to give everyone a chance to cool down. 'We just need to stand there and sway a bit, I'm no good at doing anything else anyway.'

He put out his hand again. 'Come on, Bella, you can manage that, and it's only me!'

That's right, it was only Josh. Bella clung to the thought as she relented and took his hand. Following him onto the floor, she told herself that she could hardly refuse to dance with him. He really would think something was wrong then, and there wasn't. It was only Josh.

Only Josh's arms around her. Only Josh's broad chest tantalisingly close. Only Josh's cheek resting comfortably against her hair. They had danced like this countless times before, so why was it different now? Why this sudden longing to tighten her arms around his back, to lean against him and press her face into his throat?

Bella swallowed. 'Great wedding.'

'You certainly seem to have been having a good time.' Josh sounded amused rather than jealous. 'What's with this new interest in toy boys, Bella? I've lost count of the callow youths I've seen you reduce to stammering incoherence tonight! You realise you've spoilt them for life,' he went on cheerfully. 'They're going to be dreaming about finding a woman like you for years to come, and most of them are going to end up disappointed. You ought to come with a health warning for young men!'

'It never bothered you,' said Bella, more sharply than she had intended, and Josh pulled away slightly to look at her with puzzled frown.

'It was different for me.'

'I know,' she said.

Why? she wondered. Why didn't he desire her like other men? He had never so much as hinted that he wanted her as anything more than a friend. And she would have been appalled if he had, Bella reminded herself honestly.

So why was it suddenly so hard to dance with him like this? It was if something was unravelling uncontrollably inside her, and she didn't know what it was or how to stop it. She was agonisingly conscious of him as he held her against him, not too close, but close enough to be aware of the solid strength of his body, of the warmth of his hand on her back, and the feel of his fingers curled around hers.

Terrified that she was pressing herself against him, Bella held herself stiffly. Her tongue seemed to be stuck to roof of mouth, and she felt absurdly shy of him. As the silence lengthened, she was even reduced to asking how work was going.

'Very well,' said Josh, almost as if he too was relieved at her attempt to break the increasingly tense silence. 'Things have really taken off since Aisling joined us. With her background at C.B.C.—they're our major client—she's been incredibly useful, as she knows how both organisations work.'

'Really?' said Bella, trying to force some interest into her voice.

'There's a possibility of a big contract coming up. It could be the one that changes everything for us.'

'Why is it so important?'

'It would mean expanding internationally,' Josh told her. 'C.B.C. are based in Paris, but they've got subsidiary offices around the world. We did some work for head office recently, and now they want us to implement the same training system globally.'

Bella perked up a bit, impressed in spite of herself. 'That sounds cool.'

'It might be "cool", but every national office has a lot of independence, and most are very resistant to the idea of trainers being parachuted in from head office. In some countries it's vital to establish a personal relationship with the senior executives before you start doing business.'

'You can hardly go around the world introducing yourself to every office!'

'Quite,' he agreed in a dry voice, 'but once a year C.B.C. invite the most successful executives and partners on an all-expenses-paid holiday. It's mainly intended as a social occasion and a reward for high-achievers, but it also ensures they all share in the same company ethic.'

'I'd share the ethics of any company that sent me on an all-expenses-paid holiday,' said Bella, glad that the conversation seemed to be distracting her somewhat from the pulse that beat in Josh's throat, right where she would most like to rest her face.

'That's my Bella, ever the moralist!'

Bella tore her eyes from his pulse. 'So where do they do all this bonding?'

'It's in the Seychelles this year. They're taking over a hotel on one of the small islands, and C.B.C. suggested that I go along. They think it would be a good opportunity to meet a lot of those people I may have to deal with on a social basis.'

Only Josh could sound glum about being offered a free trip to the Seychelles!

'Are you going to go?'

He lifted his shoulders as well as he could given that he had one arm round her waist and the other was holding her hand. 'Those kinds of corporate jaunts aren't really my thing,' he said, 'but Aisling thinks I should go.'

Surprise, surprise, was Bella's first jaundiced thought. 'I suppose she'll be going as well?'

'Yes.' If Josh noticed the acid tinge to her voice, he gave no sign of it. 'She's the one with all the contacts and she says it's important for me to meet people and talk about what we can do for them.'

'Really?' said Bella again, this time with a distinct layer of frost. For years now, she had been telling him that he needed to network if he wanted his company to take off, but he had never listened to *her* when she suggested that he needed to go out and meet people.

At least that unsettling urge to turn her face into his and press her lips against his jaw was receding, which was something of a relief. Getting cross seemed to be an excellent cure for *that*, anyway.

'I'm sure Aisling's right,' she said coolly, 'but I'm not sure I can see you on a beach holiday.'

'God, no.' Josh shuddered at the thought. 'I'd go mad if I had nothing to do but sit in the sun all day, but Aisling says these events are always activity-based.'

'Oh?' Bella was getting a bit sick of hearing what Aisling said.

'It's not dissimilar from the way we work with people on expeditions to build up teamwork and trust,' he said. 'Activities like diving or climbing or bush-walking are an excellent way for staff from different offices to get to know each other and bond at a more than superficial level. When you're all being challenged, you've got to be able to communicate.'

'So you're always saying,' said Bella, who had never had any trouble communicating from a sofa with a phone in her hand.

Josh grinned. 'I know your idea of the great outdoors doesn't extend beyond a veranda, but other people get a lot out of being pushed to do things they've never done before.'

'That'll be schmoozing a room for you,' said Bella tartly. 'What else is on offer?'

'I'm not sure. Aisling's keen to go scuba-diving, and there'll probably be sailing as well, so I might not be too bored.'

She sighed. It all sounded a bit too hearty for her. 'What's wrong with lying on warm white sand?' she asked. 'You can network just as effectively at a beach bar, you know.'

'We don't all have your ability to forge intimate bonds over a pina colada,' said Josh.

'It's a lot more useful than being able to dive. How much networking can you do underwater? It's just a lot of pointing and blowing bubbles.'

'You being such an expert on diving!'

'I've seen it on telly,' said Bella a little sulkily.

Josh laughed. 'You just don't like the idea of getting your hair wet. Luckily, Aisling isn't quite such a princess in these matters!'

Of course not. Aisling would tie her hair up sensibly, wear practical clothes and leave her high heels behind.

Good luck to her, thought Bella sourly. If she wanted to spend a week underwater in a rubber suit with a tank on her back when she could have a soft tropical beach and a warm lagoon and a long, cool drink brought to her lounger on a tray, that was her problem!

'By the way,' said Josh, swinging Bella round in what was for him a nifty bit of footwork, 'did you get a chance to talk to Phoebe?'

He had tightened his arm around her so that she didn't lose her balance as she swung, and it was enough to make every nerve in Bella's body jump to attention. Her heart did an odd sort of flip-flop and then settled with a thud that left her momentarily breathless.

'Talk to Phoebe?' she echoed, struggling to sound normal.

'About Aisling moving in to the house.'

'Oh, yes. Yes, I did.' Bella took a steadying breath.

She wished the music would stop and that Josh would let her go. It might be easier to concentrate then.

'What did she say?'

For a treacherous moment Bella wondered if she could throw the blame onto Phoebe, but she knew that wouldn't be fair. 'She left it up to me,' she told Josh the truth instead. 'But to be honest I think I'd like to keep the house to myself for a while.'

There, that sounded reasonable enough, didn't it? More tactful anyway than 'I'd rather stick pins in my eyes than share a house with Aisling,' which was the alternative.

'Fair enough,' said Josh. 'Aisling will be disappointed, though. She thought you would get on really well together.'

'Did she?'

'Yes, she likes you a lot.'

Bella didn't believe *that* for a minute. Aisling might smile sweetly, but her green eyes had always held a distinctly cool look. Bella had a fair idea it was a pretty accurate reflection of her own expression when the two of them met.

'Really?' she said in what she hoped was a suitably neutral tone.

'Oh, yes.' Josh nodded. 'She's told me so several times.'

Oh, well, if he was going to believe everything Aisling *said*…!

How naïve could you get? Bella wondered. She would have expected Josh to be more perceptive. He must be really besotted with Aisling if he believed every word she said. The thought was profoundly depressing somehow.

To Bella's intense relief, the music ended just then, and Josh let her go. 'I hope she'll find somewhere else soon,' she said, feeling more in control of herself and thinking she had better make the effort to be pleasant. 'I'm sure there are more convenient places than Tooting, in any case.'

'Perhaps you're right.' Josh didn't seem unduly perturbed. 'She can move in with me in the meantime anyway. You couldn't get more convenient than that!'

'What?' Bella stopped dead in dismay.

'Well, she's got to live somewhere,' he pointed out reasonably. 'She has to move out of her current flat at the end of next week, and she won't have anywhere else to go.'

'But you never wanted anyone living with you before!' Josh was famously solitary.

He shrugged. 'Aisling's different. She's a very special lady. We get on really well, and we've got a lot in common.'

Bella felt sick. Now look what she had done! 'You don't think it'll be a bit much, living and working together?'

'We won't know until we try, will we? It hasn't been a problem keeping our professional and private relationships separate so far. I think it'll work out fine.'

So that was that.

Bella couldn't believe how disastrously her refusal to share the house with Aisling had backfired. She had never dreamt that Josh was serious enough to ask Aisling to move in with him! He had always guarded his privacy so carefully. Previous girlfriends might spend the weekend with him, but he had never asked them if they wanted to leave so much as a toothbrush.

And now here he was, sharing his flat and his life with Aisling, of all people!

Bella didn't like it. Before, she had always known when she could find Josh on his own, but now he was with Aisling all the time. As the weeks after Kate's wedding passed, she saw him less and less often. When she did, she looked for signs that he was feeling crowded, or to hear that Aisling was moving into her own place, but she had to admit that they both seemed perfectly happy.

And she had no one to blame but herself. Bella could see that quite clearly. She had pushed them into living together, and now she was just going to have to accept the situation.

She didn't have to like it, though. And she missed Josh. She missed him terribly. Just his friendship, of course, she reassured herself, but still, it was a big gap in her life.

For a while she pinned her hopes on Will. She convinced herself that everything would be different when he came back from Hong Kong. Absence would work its usual miracle and the moment she saw him again she would realise just how much he meant to her.

Only it wasn't like that. She was pleased to see him, and they got on well, but something had changed. Will could see it as clearly as she did.

'I'm sorry,' she said miserably. 'It's not you. I don't know what's wrong with me.'

'Hey, don't worry about it,' said Will, who was turning out to be a real sweetie. Bella had never appreciated him properly before. 'We can still be friends.'

In some ways, Will took over Josh's role, although he could never know her as well as Josh did. Bella knew it wouldn't be long before he found someone else—he was too good-looking to stay single for long—but in the meantime they got on much better than when they had been a couple.

Her life was much quieter than it had been before...before *what*? All Bella knew was that she didn't feel like going to parties any more for some reason, and that now she preferred meeting friends for a quiet drink or going to see a film.

The theatre had never held any interest for her before either, but when Will said that he had managed to get a couple of tickets for the newest and most spectacular show in town, she actually found herself looking forward to it instead of rolling her eyes and wishing they were going to the hottest new club.

She met Will in the foyer of the theatre and together they climbed the sweeping staircases to the main bar. The room was crowded with theatre-goers anxious to get a drink before the curtain went up. Together they pushed their way through to the bar, only to come face to face with Josh and Aisling, who had managed to get their drinks and were heading out of the throng.

Bella's heart jerked horribly when she saw Josh, and she plucked frantically at Will's sleeve to catch his attention.

Josh, on the other hand, was unaffectedly pleased to see her. 'Bella! Where have you been hiding yourself?'

Clearly *his* heart wasn't somersaulting sickeningly around in his chest at the sight of her, and it cost him nothing to lean forward, still grasping both drinks, to kiss her cheek.

'I haven't seen you for ages!' he said, and then his eyes fell on Will and his face hardened. 'Oh,' he said flatly. 'You're back, are you?'

Will was rather taken aback by his tone. 'Back?'

'According to Bella, you were single-handedly saving the global economy in Hong Kong while the rest of us mere mortals were at Kate's wedding.'

'I wouldn't say that,' said Will modestly, 'but we did manage to brush through that particular crisis.'

'When did you get back?' Josh's tone was unfriendly, and he was eyeing Will like a dog with its hackles up.

'Some time ago—'

'I'm sorry we haven't been in touch—' Bella interrupted, putting her arm around Will's waist and leaning winsomely into him '—but you know what it's like when one of you has been away.' She gave him a meaningful squeeze. 'We haven't seen anybody really, have we, darling?'

Will's expression flickered, but he rose to the occasion wonderfully and put his arm around her and agreed that they hadn't felt like being very social.

'I'm glad everything's going well for you,' said Josh, not looking in the slightest bit glad, and not sounding it either.

'Oh, yes, everything's perfect,' cooed Bella. 'Isn't it, Will?'

'Perfect,' he echoed, somewhat woodenly.

'Anyway, enough about us! How are things with you two?' Bella asked brightly.

Josh handed Aisling her drink so that he could put his free arm around her in imitation of the way Will and Bella were standing. 'We're great,' he said.

Did Bella imagine it, or was that a defensive edge to his voice?

'It's not like you to come to the theatre, Bella,' Aisling put in. 'Josh was just saying that you've always been too much of a drama queen yourself to ever want to watch anyone else getting all the attention on stage!'

Bella could imagine Josh saying that, but not in the way Aisling made it sound. 'No, well, I'm rather surprised to see you two here as well,' she countered sweetly. 'I thought you preferred being outdoors, competing as to who has the muddiest boots or the dirtiest towel.'

'We like being active,' Aisling agreed, her smile every bit as fixed as Bella's. 'But we enjoy culture too.'

Josh didn't look as if he was enjoying himself. Bella raised her brows, but before she could retort, Will had tugged at her. 'If you want that drink, Bella, we'd better get going.'

'Of course.' Bella smiled sweetly at Josh and Aisling. 'See you later!'

'*Culture!*' she exploded the moment they were out of earshot. 'It's only a musical! And Josh will hate it!'

'So, do you want to tell me what that was all about?' said Will when he had caught the barmaid's attention and could hand Bella a gin and tonic.

Bella didn't pretend not to know what he was talking about. 'I didn't want Josh to know that we've split up.'

'I gathered that,' he said dryly.

'Thanks for playing along,' she told him.

Will looked at her curiously. 'I thought Josh was your big buddy?' he said. 'I assumed he'd be the first person you would tell if you split up.'

'Normally he would be,' admitted Bella, 'but he was so unpleasant about you at Kate's wedding that it made me cross, and besides—'

'Besides what?' asked Will when she stopped.

'Nothing.' She couldn't explain why it had seemed such a good idea at the time to let Josh believe that she was still madly in love with Will.

Will raised his brows. 'It must be six weeks since Kate got married. Do you mean to say that he still doesn't know?'

'I just haven't had an opportunity to tell him,' said Bella, swirling her gin defensively.

'You did more than not tell him just now,' he pointed out. 'You went out of your way to make him think that we were still very much together!'

'I know,' she said guiltily. 'I just can't stand the thought of Aisling feeling sorry for me. You saw what she was like. She'd be all warm and sympathetic and oh-so-slightly smug because she and Josh are so cosy together.' Bella grimaced at the thought and took a slug of gin. 'You know they're living together now?'

'Ah,' said Will.

Bella lowered her glass suspiciously. 'What's that supposed to mean?'

'It explains why you're so upset.'

'I'm not upset,' she said with something of a snap. 'I just don't like Aisling. Josh and I were fine until she came along.'

'But it's not Aisling who's the problem, is it? It's you.'

'Me?'

'You're in love with Josh.'

Bella opened her mouth to deny it vehemently. She was fully intending to tell Will that he didn't know what he was talking about, and that there was no *question* of being in love with Josh, who was just her dear friend and absolutely nothing else.

But somehow the words wouldn't come out. Instead she felt a peculiar sinking sensation, as if she were teetering at edge of a cliff, not daring to look down at what lay in the abyss below. Closing her mouth, she swallowed hard.

'I'm right, aren't I?' said Will, as the bell warning the audience to take their seats sounded.

Smiling ruefully, he took Bella's glass from her nerveless hand and set it on a nearby table. Then he took her arm and propelled her towards the stairs. 'Poor Bella. You look like you've been hit by a truck!'

That was exactly how Bella felt. Numbly, she let Will guide her up the stairs and into her seat. Having resisted it for so long, now the truth was staring her in the face, she couldn't avoid it and she felt suddenly, horribly afraid.

How could it have happened? She had never loved Josh before, or at least not in this new, scary way, and there was no reason for her to start falling in love with him now.

Bella didn't want to be in love with him. She wanted to go back to the way they had been before, but the certainty that she could never do that now was cold around her heart. As long as she had refused to acknowledge it, things were OK, but Will's careless words had been all that were needed to let the genie out of the bottle, and now she could never get it back.

The truth was out there now, implacable, undeniable. After all these years, she was in love with Josh.

CHAPTER THREE

BELLA stared unseeingly at the dancers on the stage and remembered what Phoebe had said to her at Kate's wedding. 'You'll know when you find him,' she had said.

But she hadn't known. It had taken Will, not normally the most perceptive of men, to point out the obvious, and now her life had changed for ever.

What was she going to do? Always before when she hadn't known what to do she had talked to Josh, but he was the one person now she couldn't, *mustn't*, tell.

If sleeping together all those years ago would have spoilt their friendship, it was nothing to what confessing how she felt now would do. Josh was with Aisling, Bella reminded herself bleakly. She was just going to have to accept that friends was all they were, and make an effort to like Aisling for his sake.

That wasn't going to be easy, but she would try.

She might not be able to tell Josh how her life had changed so completely, but she could tell him the truth about Will. It was stupid to carry on pretending, Bella decided. She had never lied to Josh before, and it didn't feel right. If they were friends, and they had always been that, she should just admit that Will was not her ideal man after all.

But there never seemed to be an opportunity over the next couple of weeks. In spite of her determination to try harder with Aisling, Bella balked at trying to explain why she had pretended the way she had in front of her. She wasn't sure she could stand Aisling's sympathy or—worse—her understanding.

So when she got an email from Josh one day saying that Aisling was going out with some old colleagues and suggesting that the two of them meet up for a drink the following evening, Bella thought it would be her best chance to straighten things out. Some of them, anyway.

'Absolutely,' she emailed back. 'Don't seem to have had a good chat for ages and have lots to tell you. Usual time, usual place?'

'News for you too,' Josh replied immediately. 'See you tomorrow.'

Bella was ridiculously nervous next day, and so tense and snappy at work that others in the office took to edging round her. Really, it was worse than going on a first date!

She couldn't believe that she felt this twitchy about meeting Josh. She was pinning her hopes on a miraculous cure, whereby one look at him would be enough for her to realise that she had blown everything out of proportion—and, let's face it, it wouldn't be the first time she had done *that*!—and to discover that she wasn't in love with him at all.

But part of her knew that this was just wishful thinking. She was stuck with this now.

Her hands shook as she brushed her hair and put on fresh lipstick in the ladies' loo at the end of the day.

'You look nice,' said her boss's PA, who was also titivating in front of the mirror prior to going out. 'Heavy date tonight?'

'No,' said Bella, moistening her lips. 'Just meeting a friend.'

A *friend*. That was all he was. She must remember that. Never mind that she couldn't even say his name without her insides twisting themselves into a knot.

She arrived at the bar ten minutes early, unheard of for her. It was a standing joke that her watch ran twenty-five minutes slower than Josh's. She got herself a drink and sat down at a table, twisting the glass nervously between her hands.

This was awful! She didn't know whether she longed for Josh to arrive or dreaded it.

When he did, bang on time as usual, he didn't even bother to look for her, but glanced at his watch, assumed she would be late and went straight to the bar.

Bella's heart jerked painfully at the sight of him and stuck, hammering frantically, in her throat. It was lucky that he hadn't seen her and come straight over, as she couldn't have spoken if she had tried. So much for her hope that she would turn out not to be in love with him after all.

Her eyes rested on him hungrily as he stood at the bar, wearing chinos and a battered old jacket. She had spent years rolling her eyes at his complete absence of any sense of style at all, and the boring way he insisted on having his hair cut. Now just looking at the back of his neck was like a hand squeezing hard inside her.

Josh might not be the sharpest of dressers but he exuded a kind of tough competence, and he wasn't a man who got ignored by bar staff. He was served far more quickly than Bella had been, and turned with a beer in his hand to look for a table.

Swallowing hard, Bella waved to attract his attention, and his searching expression changed ludicrously to one of surprise.

'Bella!' He put his beer down on the table and bent to kiss her cheek. 'You're on time! Did I slip into a parallel universe without noticing? What's come over you?'

I'm in love with you.

Her face tingled where his lips had brushed against her skin. She felt absurdly shy.

'Things were quiet at work so I left early,' she said.

'Things quiet in the PR world?' said Josh as he sat down opposite her. 'This *is* a parallel universe!'

He picked up his beer. 'Cheers,' he said and they chinked glasses. Taking a sip he set the glass down again and smiled at Bella. 'So,' he said. 'You're looking good.'

'So are you.'

He looked more than good. He looked wonderful. Bella couldn't take her eyes off him. She wanted to crawl over to him, sit in his lap and run her hand up his arm and along his shoulder, to kiss his throat and then work her way along his jaw to his mouth...

Appalled at the sheer grip of lust, she gulped her wine shakily. All those years she had taken Josh for granted, and now she could hardly keep her hands off him! Thank God he was sitting opposite and hadn't chosen the seat beside her. Even so, she tightened both hands around the stem of the glass where she could see them on top of the table and keep them under control.

'How are things with you?' she managed.

'Great. And you?'

'Yes, fine.'

This was ghastly. Bella felt close to tears. It had always been so easy with Josh before. They would get their drinks and spend the rest of the evening talking and laughing and teasing each other, and now they were sitting here being *polite* to each other.

'Are you still going off to the Seychelles?'

Josh nodded. He was obviously picking up on the awkward atmosphere. 'In a couple of weeks,' he said.

'Lucky you. I wish I could go away in November. It's always so dark and miserable then.'

God, now they were reduced to the weather!

Josh didn't even try and pick up on that particular conversational gambit. He drank his beer instead and an uncomfortable silence fell.

Bella concentrated on making patterns with the condensation on the bottom of her glass. She was supposed to be telling him about Will but she wasn't sure how to do it without explaining how her feelings had changed, and if Josh probed too far in that direction it wouldn't take him long to realise that she had changed, and then he would want to know why and…oh, God, perhaps it would be better not to say anything?

'So,' said Josh again, sounding rather strained. 'What's new with you? You said you had a lot to tell me.'

'You go first,' she said quickly. 'You said you had news too.'

'Yes…yes, I do.'

He sounded almost as hesitant as she felt. He obviously didn't know where to begin either. A tiny chill crept into Bella's stomach.

'Is it good or bad?' she asked, trying to make light of it.

'Good,' said Josh after another tiny hesitation.

'You don't sound very sure!'

He didn't. Josh could hear it himself. 'No, it is good. Definitely good,' he said.

The best, in fact. So why didn't it feel fantastic? Josh wondered. It had seemed such a good idea when Aisling suggested it. More than that, it had made perfect sense. He should be standing on the table, shouting his luck to the world.

He just hadn't expected it to be so difficult to tell Bella, that was all.

She was looking at him curiously across the table. 'Is it something to do with work?'

'No, no, nothing like that.' Josh took another desperate drink of his beer.

Bella pursed her lips, rolled her eyes and shook back her long, blonde hair in an achingly familiar gesture of exasperation. 'Well?' she demanded, sounding like the old Bella, and not the strange new, shy, prompt Bella who had been sitting opposite him a moment ago. 'Do I have to guess, or are you going to tell me?'

'Aisling and I are getting married.'

Josh winced as he heard how he blurted out the words as if he felt guilty or something. He had meant to lead up to it more gently.

He looked at Bella, unsure of how she would react. She seemed to have frozen, and for a second or two her expression was completely blank. Then the blue eyes dropped to her wine and she stared at it for a few moments, until Josh began to wonder if she had heard him.

'Bella?' he asked, but she had already lifted her gaze and there was a bright smile on her face.

'Well…congratulations!' she said in a voice that matched her smile, and she half stood to lean across the table and kiss him on the cheek.

Her hair swung against Josh's face, and he could smell her perfume. She always wore exactly the same one. 'Allure,' she had told him when he asked once what it was, and she had grinned at him. 'Feel free to buy me a huge bottle whenever you want!' Sometimes when she had been in his flat, he could sniff the fragrance still lingering in the air. It always made him think of her.

What perfume did Aisling wear? Wasn't that the kind of thing a fiancé should know?

'When did all this happen?' she asked, sitting back

down with the same bright smile that for some reason intensified Josh's feeling of unease. But she looked just the same, the same blue eyes, the same tilting lashes, the same swing of spun gold around her face as she shook her hair out of the way.

It was just the smile that was wrong, but Josh couldn't put his finger on why.

'Last week,' he said.

They had just won a big contract, and the whole company had been out celebrating that evening. When they got home, Josh had tried to tell Aisling how much he appreciated what she had done. There was no doubt that she had made a huge difference. She had finely honed marketing skills, and with her background knowledge of clients like C.B.C. she had been able to steer the company in a new direction which was paying dividends already. This had been an important contract to win, and if they could get the C.B.C. deal as well, the future would be assured.

'We couldn't have done it without you,' he had told her, still high on the relief and euphoria of the staff. They had all worked hard but Aisling's input had been key and they all knew it. 'We make a fantastic team.'

'I think you and I make a fantastic team whatever we're doing,' Aisling had said, smiling. 'Why don't we make it permanent?'

And Josh hadn't been able to think of a reason not to. Aisling was beautiful and intelligent and she shared his interests. He knew they could live together. She didn't have any annoying habits.

Bella, for instance, would drive him mad. She would never close drawers or put the tops back on bottles and she would leave her clothes strewn all over his flat. She would clutter his streamlined bathroom with cosmetics and monopolise his phone and embark on cooking over-elaborate meals, half of which would end up in the bin.

There was nothing like that with Aisling. Josh couldn't imagine ever finding anyone who fitted into his world with so little fuss.

Everyone else was settling down. What was the point of holding out for…what? Bella was wrapped up in that pillock, Will, and if it wasn't Will it would be some other chinless wonder who worked in the City.

Bella had been telling him for years that he had no sense of romance, and Josh didn't have a problem with that. Romantics—like Bella herself—had this rosy and, in his view, completely unrealistic view about relationships. They wanted everything to be perfect, and life was never like that.

Josh was trained in survival, and that was all about adapting to different situations, about keeping your options open as long as you could and compromising when you couldn't. And when you had to make a decision, you had to make it fast and stick with it.

Aisling was right, he had told himself. They did make a good team, and if he had learnt anything from his years on expedition, being part of a good team was everything. Why not commit himself and make it permanent?

'Last week?' Bella was staring at him, the blue eyes hurt. 'Why didn't you tell me?'

'I wanted to wait and tell you on your own,' said Josh awkwardly. 'I haven't told anybody else yet.'

'Why not?'

'I wanted you to be the first to know.' He looked at her anxiously. 'I know it's a bit sudden, but what do you think?'

Bella's smile wavered a little but she took a deep breath.

'I think it's fantastic news, Josh,' she said. 'I'm so happy for you.'

'Really?'

'Of course. I'm a bit stunned, I suppose but…yes, of course I'm happy for you. I can see Aisling's perfect for you.'

'She is, isn't she?' Josh was conscious of trying to force enthusiasm into his voice. That couldn't be right, surely?

'Absolutely,' said Bella, who could feel her smile growing fixed.

'You do like her, don't you?'

'Of course,' she lied.

She could feel another silence threatening. 'So when's the wedding?' she hurried on.

'We haven't decided on a date yet.'

'Are you going to go traditional, or do something different?'

'That'll be up to Aisling,' said Josh. 'I don't think she's made any plans yet.'

Bella's jaw was beginning to feel rigid with the effort of keeping her smile in place. 'Can I be your best man? It's supposed to be your best friend, isn't it?'

Josh looked at her. 'You'll always be that, Bella,' he said.

'Well, this calls for another drink.' Bella drained her glass with an edge of desperation. 'I'll have a glass of champagne this time!'

'I'll get them.' Josh leapt to his feet. 'You stay there.'

It was such a relief to stop smiling. Bella found that she was breathing very shallowly. She was shaking, too, she realised dully. It had taken everything she had to appear pleased for Josh while inside she felt so sick and utterly desolate that she could hardly think straight.

She had known it was coming. The moment he hesitated

about telling her his news, she had sensed what it would be, but even so the savage twist of pain had caught her unawares and she had almost cried out. Instead she had had to smile, and she would have to go on smiling, whatever it cost.

Josh must never know how she felt now. He mustn't even guess. It wouldn't be fair now that he had made his choice. He would be appalled and embarrassed, and even though it wouldn't change the way he felt about Aisling, it might make him feel awkward about celebrating his engagement, and Bella wasn't prepared to do that to him.

So she put her bright smile back on when Josh came back with a bottle of champagne in an ice bucket. 'This is more like it,' she said as he eased out the cork with a typical lack of any kind of flourish and poured the champagne.

'Congratulations, Josh,' she said, picking up her glass and touching it to his.

'Thanks, Bella.' Josh's face relaxed. 'It's stupid, but I was worried about telling you.'

'You shouldn't have been. You know I just want you to be happy.'

'We'll still be friends, won't we?'

'Of course we will—but who's going to marry me now when I get to forty and no one else wants me?' Bella kept smiling to show that she was joking. 'I thought I could rely on you!'

'I can't imagine that happening,' said Josh. 'As long as I've known you there's always been a long queue of men just desperate for the chance to show you how much they want you! What about Will?'

Bella studied her champagne. 'Ah, well, there's a vacant place at the front of the queue at the moment.'

Josh's face changed and he put down his glass. 'Bella?'

'Yes, I'm afraid my news isn't quite as exciting as yours,' she said. 'Will and I split up.'

'But you seemed so happy with him. You thought he was perfect!' Josh seemed at a loss. 'What happened?'

'Oh, you know…' Bella shrugged.

'No,' said Josh. 'Tell me.'

'It was just one of those things,' she said, avoiding his eye.

She had decided to tell Josh the truth about Will, but that was before she had known that he was going to marry Aisling. Everything had changed now. If Josh thought that the decision had been a mutual one, he would start to wonder why she was so unhappy, and Bella didn't want him going *there*. He knew her much too well.

No, far better for him to think that it was Will she loved. It would explain why she wasn't herself at the moment, and it would give her a good excuse to stop smiling, which would be a huge relief.

'Will isn't ready to settle down,' she told Josh. That at least was true. There had never been any question of making things permanent. Will was no more keen to marry than Bella had been. 'He's having much too good a time being an eligible bachelor.'

Which was also true. Will had found her attractive, and she had blended nicely with his décor, but he had never really loved her. That was one reason they were able to get on so well now.

'It was all getting a bit intense for him,' she explained.

'Isn't that usually your line?' said Josh, lifting an eyebrow.

'I know. Ironic, isn't it? All those years I've spent dumping men the moment they start to crowd me, and now I'm getting a taste of my own medicine.' Bella forced a smile. 'I'm sure you're going to tell me it serves me right!'

'No, I'm going to tell you I never thought Will was good enough for you. I know you thought he was perfect, but clearly the man has no taste. You'll find someone much better,' he told her confidently.

'The trouble is that I don't want anyone better,' she said in a low voice. 'There's only one man I want.'

'Bella…' Josh frowned. 'That sounds serious.'

'I think it is.' Bella twisted her glass between her fingers, unable to look at him properly. 'Oh, I know I've fallen in and out of love before, but this is different. It's more than liking a man with a smart car who can show you a good time. This is needing someone with every tiny bit of you and wanting to be with him and be able to touch him and knowing that you've lost your chance.

'It's too late,' she finished dully.

'*Is* it too late?'

Bella lifted her eyes from her glass and looked at him, so dear and so familiar and so suddenly, unexpectedly gorgeous.

And so engaged to Aisling.

She swallowed, and nodded, all at once unable to speak.

Josh got up without a word and sat down next to her so that he could put his arm around her. 'Poor Bella,' he said gently. 'Does it hurt?'

To her horror, Bella felt a tear trickle out of the edge of her eyes, and then another. Frantically, she tried to brush them away with the back of her hand, but it only seemed to make them come faster.

'I'll get over it,' she said unsteadily.

'You have got it bad, Bel,' said Josh, tightening his arm around her, which made things even worse.

Bella longed to be able to turn her face into his throat and cling to him but she couldn't let herself relax or she would lose control completely. She would fling her arms around him, and blizzard kisses all over his face and beg him not to marry Aisling. She would tell him that he was the one she loved and needed and wanted, and implore him to kiss her back, to pull her down onto the floor and make love to her and promise that he would never let her go.

The thought of how the quiet, restrained Josh would react to such a melodramatic scene was enough to make Bella give a hiccup of laughter through her tears. Poor Josh, she could never to do that to him.

'Honestly, I'll be fine,' she said, straightening out of the comfort of his arm before she really did do something she regretted. It was one of the hardest things she had ever had to do.

She dug in her bag for a tissue and blew her nose fiercely.

'Do you want me to kill Will for you?' asked Josh. 'I will if you want.'

Bella managed a shaky smile. 'Thanks, but I don't think that would help. And it's not Will's fault,' she added, in case Josh decided to track down the unsuspecting Will and give him a piece of his mind. 'He can't help how I feel.'

'He could give you a chance.'

Bella shook her head. 'I've had my chance, and I blew it,' she said.

Absently rubbing her cheeks with the crumpled tissue, she put her smile back into place. 'I'm sorry about that,' she said, sitting up straight and squaring her shoulders. 'I didn't mean to go all tearful on you. We're supposed to be celebrating your engagement here!' She held out her glass. 'Come on, let's have some more champagne!'

Josh topped up their glasses obediently, but he was worried about Bella. At least he now knew the reason for the strain behind her bright smile.

He hadn't been entirely joking when he asked Bella if she would like him to kill Will. OK, he might not go quite as far as murder, but when he saw the pain in her blue eyes, he was gripped by such a cold rage that he almost wished that Will would walk into the bar so that he could have the satisfaction of hurting him in return. He wanted to see Will on his knees, grovelling to Bella, and preferably with a bloody nose.

What was wrong with the man anyway? Josh thought about how warm and soft she had felt as she leant against him, the silkiness of her hair under his cheek. Will needed his head examining. How could a man turn his back on Bella, with those legs and that figure and those mischievous blue eyes? Or her warmth and her humour and that dirty chuckle?

It wasn't even as if she was just an airhead. There was a lot more to Bella than that. She could be infuriatingly frivolous sometimes, but when she chose to use it she had a perfectly good brain behind that ditzy blonde façade, as Josh had frequently pointed out. Not that Bella ever took any notice of him.

Look at her now. Her face was a little flushed, and her eyes held a suspiciously manic glitter, but she was putting on a brave show to hide her broken heart. Josh wanted to reach out and hug her again, but he had sensed a certain resistance before, as if she was only holding herself in with an effort.

And it wasn't his arms she wanted around her, was it?

'We must have a party to celebrate your engagement,' Bella was saying, and his mouth turned down at the corners.

'You know I'm not a big party person.'

'All right,' she conceded. 'What about a dinner, like we did for Phoebe and for Kate when they got engaged? It'll make quite a change to celebrate a real engagement rather than a pretend one! Do you think Aisling would like that?'

Aisling! Josh was startled to realise that he had forgotten about Aisling there for a few minutes.

'Yes…yes, I'm sure she would,' he said awkwardly.

'Good, that's settled then. Shall we go for next week-end? I'll talk to Phoebe and to Kate and I'll email you with a date.' Bella lifted her glass to him. 'Cheers,' she said.

It was her own fault for not recognising how important Josh was to her sooner. Bella could hardly bear to think now about all the years when she had peacocked around, always with some gorgeous man in tow, taking it for granted that Josh would be there when she got bored or wanted comfort or a laugh.

Well, now he was there for someone else, and she would just have to endure it. Aisling had seen in Josh everything that she had been standing too close to see. Had been too silly and self-absorbed to see.

That Josh was a man, not the boy she remembered. That he was quiet and competent and self-contained. That his eyes gleamed with humour. That his hands were square and strong, and his body hard and his cool mouth could tie you up in knots just by thinking about it.

He had been the best of friends to her for so long, and now she would be the same to him, Bella vowed. She would keep her feelings to herself, and be happy for him, and pull out all the stops to celebrate his engagement.

She planned a spectacular meal that no one would ever forget, and then had to ring up Kate and beg her to come and help her before everyone else arrived.

'Does it have to be quite so over-the-top?' Kate asked,

raising her brows as she studied the menu Bella had drawn up after poring over recipe books for days.

'I want it to be memorable.'

'It'll certainly be that if you can pull it off! A croquembouche! What's that?'

'A big pile of profiteroles filled with cream. It's supposed to be held together with spun sugar, but I thought I'd pour over chocolate instead,' said Bella. 'Only it doesn't seem to have worked very well.'

Glumly she contemplated her profiteroles which she had spent hours making the night before. The light-as-air little choux buns shown in the recipe book had ended up like pancakes. Stuffing them with cream was going to be a nightmare. They lay turgidly on a plate, not so much a pile as a mess.

'Hmmnn.' Kate studied them, unimpressed, and then went back to the menu without further comment. 'What else? Canapés, individual soufflés, beef Wellington...! You couldn't have picked at least one uncomplicated dish?'

Bella sighed. 'It seemed like a good idea at the time.'

'Josh would be just as happy with a tin of baked beans.'

'I know,' she said, restacking recipe books to try and clear the decks a bit. 'But he needs to know that I've made a special effort for Aisling.'

Kate pulled an apron over her head and tied the strings behind her back. 'Because you hate the fact that he's marrying her.'

'Yes—no!' Bella corrected herself hastily, hearing what she had said, and then she stopped, realising there was no point in trying to fool Kate. 'I suppose it's obvious?'

'It is to us, lovey. We've known you a long time.'

Bella bit her lip. 'Josh has known me a long time too.'

'Yes, but it'll be different for him. I know he can be

incredibly perceptive sometimes, but he's still a man,' said Kate kindly. 'He probably hasn't got a clue that you don't like Aisling.'

'No,' said Bella, remembering how sure he had been at Kate's wedding that she and Aisling would get on. 'I don't want him to know that, though. He'd be really hurt.'

'Don't you think Aisling is right for him?'

'Do you?'

Kate considered, her head tilted to one side. 'I can't quite believe he's going to marry her at all,' she admitted at last. 'I suppose Phoebe and I always assumed that you and Josh would end up together.'

Bella was glad of the fact that she had her back to Kate as she opened the fridge in search of mushrooms. She had her expression under control by the time she turned back and pulled out a chopping board.

'It's too late for that now,' she said, and was proud of the careless note in her voice.

Kate took the board and the mushrooms and began chopping pensively. 'Maybe Josh won't marry her after all.'

'I don't see that happening,' said Bella. 'You know what Josh is like. His word is his bond and all that. If he's decided to marry Aisling, then he will.'

'Aisling might change *her* mind,' Kate suggested hopefully.

But there was no sign of Aisling changing her mind when she and Josh arrived for the celebration dinner. She was looking stunning in a sheath dress, and was full of wedding plans as she flashed her diamond ring around.

'It's lovely,' said Bella, admiring it dutifully.

'Josh took me to the jeweller's at the weekend. It took me hours to decide which one I wanted, didn't it, Josh?'

'Hours,' he agreed somewhat thinly.

Aisling gave a silvery peal of laughter and hugged his arm. 'Poor Josh! He was getting a bit bored at the end. You know what he's like, Bella!'

Bella handed her a glass of champagne without looking at Josh. 'Yes,' she said. 'I know what he's like.'

CHAPTER FOUR

'I'M AFRAID it was terribly expensive,' Aisling was bur-
bling on, 'but he *did* say I could have whichever one I
liked best.'

'I'm sure he thinks you're worth it,' said Bella evenly.

Pouring another glass, she gave it to Josh, forcing herself to meet his eyes. 'I know you'd rather have a beer,
but I'm afraid champagne is obligatory on these occasions!'

'Thanks.' Josh took the glass from her, but Bella was
so on edge that as their fingers brushed, she jerked her
hand away as if from an electric shock, and half the champagne spilt onto the floor.

'Sorry,' she muttered, scarlet-cheeked, and when she
topped up his glass, her hand holding the bottle was not
quite steady.

'Are you OK?' he asked in concern.

'I'm fine. Just a bit nervous about the meal,' she offered
as an explanation. 'I've been a bit too ambitious, I think.'

Josh's face relaxed into a grin. 'You always do this,
Bella. You plan these incredibly elaborate menus and then
get into a state when they don't work out. I wish you'd
throw all those recipe books away and stick to offering
your guests cheese on toast!'

'I might do after tonight,' she said, a reluctant smile
tugging at her mouth and as their eyes met it was as if the
two of them were alone for a tiny moment in a private
world.

Josh was the first to look away. 'It's good of you to

have gone to so much effort,' he said looking around the kitchen.

'Yes, it all looks lovely,' said Aisling, who had observed the way their eyes had locked with a narrowed gaze.

Bella had found an antique damask cloth for the old pine table where she and Kate and Phoebe had spent so many hours drinking wine and putting the world to rights, and she was pleased with the effect now that it was laid with gleaming glasses and flowers and lit candles.

It all looked just as romantic as she had intended—if you looked one way, at least. The effect was rather spoiled if you looked the other by all the dirty dishes piled up beside the sink. She had used just about every implement in the kitchen already and there was still so much to do. She had always loved the big cosy kitchen, but sometimes you could see the point of a separate dining room where you could pretend everything was under control.

'I do like this kitchen,' Aisling was saying. 'It's the main reason I was hoping to move in at one time.'

'I'm sorry,' said Bella, remembering how she had turned down the idea when Josh had suggested it.

She swallowed. That brief, intense exchange of looks had left her feeling peculiar, almost jarred, as if she had stumbled in the dark. You weren't supposed to gaze into a man's eyes when you were just friends, and especially not when you were celebrating his engagement to someone else.

'I must have seemed very unfriendly when I insisted on keeping the house to myself,' she said by way of an apology.

'Don't worry about it,' said Aisling, waving a careless hand so that the diamond on her finger glinted in the candlelight. 'I'm sure I'd have felt exactly the same. And anyway, as things turned out it was best thing that could have happened, wasn't it, darling?'

She took Josh's arm in a proprietorial manner. 'If you'd agreed to let me come here, I wouldn't have moved in with Josh, and we would never have discovered just how compatible we were,' she said. 'We probably wouldn't even have thought of getting married, would we, Josh?'

'It's hard to know,' he said.

'So it's all thanks to you, Bella.' Aisling lifted her glass with the hand that wasn't clutching Josh and sent her a glittering smile. 'Thank you!'

Bella's own smile was feeling more than a little fixed, and she turned away to pick up a plate. 'Have a canapé,' she said.

'Ooh, I shouldn't really…' Aisling inspected the plate. Bella was proud of her way with nibbles, and she had spent hours making these look spectacular with exquisite garnishes.

'These are the only part of the meal that have worked, so I should make the most of them if I were you,' she told Aisling.

'Well, maybe just one.' Aisling let go of Josh and her hand hovered over the plate until she had selected the one she evidently judged the least fattening. 'Delicious,' she said.

'Have another.'

'Oh, no, thanks.' She patted her perfectly flat stomach complacently. 'I've seen the perfect dress already but I can't afford to put on so much as a milligram if I want to get into it for the wedding.'

'Have you decided when it's going to be?'

Bella was hugely grateful to Phoebe for coming up and joining in the conversation just then. Possibly she had seen that Bella herself was close to taking her canapés and shoving them down Aisling's ample cleavage.

'Next May,' said Aisling. 'I think a spring wedding is lovely, don't you?'

There was a feverish glitter in Aisling's green eyes and she seemed on a high. Bella supposed she couldn't blame her. She would be euphoric if she were wearing Josh's ring and had Josh to go home with at the end of the evening, but she hadn't anticipated that every word Aisling spoke would be like a knife twisting inside her.

'Excuse me,' she said, suddenly desperate to get out of the kitchen so no one could see her face. 'I must just go and see about the starter.'

Phoebe was listening to Aisling's increasingly manic wedding plans, and Josh looked down into his champagne with a slight frown.

'Don't worry,' Gib said in his ear. 'I brought some beer with me.' He peered into his own glass with a grimace. 'I don't know why women insist on drinking this stuff! Down that, and I'll get you a proper drink.'

Josh grinned and drained his glass obediently. Gib could always make things seem better.

The meal couldn't be described as a culinary triumph—Bella's never were—but there was plenty of wine and good company. While Aisling was on extra sparkling form, Bella was much quieter than usual, but once she stopped jumping up and down to see to the food she did relax, and it was a great evening.

When she got up much later to make some more coffee, Josh followed her to the working end of the kitchen to give her a hand while the others carried on a spirited argument at the table.

'In case I don't get a chance to say it later, thank you,' he said.

'Sorry about the beef,' she sighed. 'And the pudding. It was all a bit of a disaster, wasn't it?'

'It was delicious,' Josh lied manfully. 'And anyway, it doesn't matter what the food was like. What matters is all the trouble you went to. It's been a very special evening, and I really appreciate it. So does Aisling,' he added as he put his arms around Bella and gave her a hug.

For a second or so she leant into him, but then pulled away and made a big deal of filling the kettle.

'Still no word from Will?' Josh asked.

'I see him occasionally,' she said, carefully spooning coffee into the cafetière, 'but it's not the same.'

'Isn't it getting any easier?'

Bella stopped and looked straight at him. 'No,' she said.

Right, she was going to have to get on with her life, Bella told herself the next morning as she tackled the monumental pile of washing up. Oh, for a dishwasher!

Miracles were not going to happen. Aisling was hell-bent on marrying Josh, and judging by the conversation at dinner last night had turned overnight into an obsessive who could talk about nothing else. They had heard all about Aisling's plans for the wedding, some of which were clearly news to Josh, and had even been treated to a summary of every possible honeymoon location.

'We're off to the Seychelles in a couple of weeks anyway,' Aisling rattled on, 'so we can check it out and see if it's a place we'd want to go back to. It looks beautiful, but there might not be enough to do there apart from diving.'

'Most honeymoon couples don't have any problem finding something to do!' said Gib, amused, but Aisling took him seriously.

'Josh and I aren't like that. We need to be able to climb

or sail or go white-water rafting. We'd both be bored to death lying on a beach all day.'

Bella had been unable to resist exchanging a speaking glance with Kate and Phoebe.

'Not one of us!' Kate had mouthed back.

'She's protesting too much if you ask me,' Phoebe had murmured in Bella's ear a bit later. 'Bet she hates all that tough stuff really.'

Bella didn't think Phoebe was right. Aisling might have rattled on obsessively about weddings all night, but she was equally at home out in the wild like Josh, and once the wedding of the century—as theirs was clearly intended to be—was over, she would settle down and be good for Josh.

Which meant that *she* had to get a grip. No more misery, no more longing for Josh or dreaming that things could be different. It was time to restart her life.

Easier said than done. Bella did try. She made herself go to parties again, and she tried to keep herself busy the rest of the time so that she didn't have too much time to think, but the thought of Josh was like a constant ache inside her. It was the first thing Bella was aware of when she woke, and the last thing before she went to sleep, and in between it throbbed dully and insistently and made it impossible to think of anything else.

She lost weight, which didn't suit her, and she knew that her skin looked tired and there were dark shadows under her eyes. Kate and Phoebe tutted in concern when they saw her.

'You look awful!'

'Thanks!'

'Seriously, Bella, you're not sickening for something, are you?'

Only with love, thought Bella drearily.

'I'm just tired,' she said. 'I need a holiday, but I can't afford to go anywhere. My last credit card bill was so enormous I thought I was going to pass out when I opened it. I wish someone would offer *me* a free week in the Seychelles,' she sighed.

The thought of a week with nothing to do but lie on a tropical beach was incredibly inviting. No diving, no sailing, just lying there with your eyes closed…yes, she could handle that!

'It would be nice, wouldn't it?' said Kate. 'It's all right for Josh and Aisling!'

'When are they off?' Phoebe asked, getting up to freshen their glasses.

'Soon, I think.'

'I haven't seen them since your dinner. How is Josh?'

Bella's throat tightened at the mere sound of his name. 'I don't know,' she said as casually as she could. 'I haven't seen him either.'

Phoebe frowned. 'I hope nothing's wrong. It doesn't sound like Josh to drop out of sight like that. Hasn't he been in touch at all?'

'He rang and left a message thanking me for the dinner,' Bella admitted, 'but it wasn't the kind of message that needed a reply, so I didn't.'

'But Bella, he'd expect you to call him back anyway, wouldn't he?'

She hunched a shoulder, unable to explain how hard she found the idea of talking to Josh now. 'I didn't want to intrude,' she said defensively. 'They probably just want to be alone at the moment.'

'They probably think you're ignoring them,' said Kate, sounding unusually astringent. 'I thought you wanted to make Josh think that you liked Aisling?'

'I do...I just need a little time to get used to the idea of him getting married,' she confessed.

'You've had nearly three weeks, Bella,' said Phoebe gently as she handed her back her glass. 'You're going to have to come to terms with it some time.'

Bella sighed and sipped her drink. 'I know.'

The trouble was that she couldn't imagine having a normal conversation with Josh now when all she could think of to say was I love you, I love you, I love you. She *could* ring and wish them a good trip, she supposed bleakly. At least it would give them something to talk about.

'I'll call him,' she promised.

To her relief, her friends let the matter drop then. 'I'm not sure we can run to a week in the Seychelles, but what else can we do to cheer you up?' asked Kate. 'It's Friday tomorrow. Why don't you come round and have supper with us? You look as if you could do with a decent meal.'

'I'd like to, but I'm supposed to be going to some party in Battersea,' Bella said without enthusiasm.

By the time she got home from work the next day she felt even less enthusiastic about the prospect. It was a vile November evening, and her umbrella had been useless in the gusty wind. The walk from the tube was enough to leave her wet and bedraggled, and she wasn't sure she could face tarting herself up, going out into the rain again and spending the evening smiling and looking as if she was having fun.

But the alternative was to sit at home missing Josh and trying not to cry.

Maybe a drink would perk her up? Bella made herself a vodka and tonic and slumped on the kitchen sofa, not noticeably perked but appreciating the drink anyway. She was still trying to summon up the energy to have a shower when the doorbell rang.

Drink in hand, she went out to peer through the peephole, and her heart did an alarming somersault when she saw Josh standing on the other side of the door, huddled into his coat, with the collar turned up. His hair was plastered to his head, and the rain was running down his face.

'Josh!' Hastily Bella opened the door and stared at him. 'What are you doing here?'

'I needed to see you.'

Josh hadn't thought about what he was going to say. He had just followed his instinct which was to get to Bella. He couldn't explain on the phone, he had wanted her presence, and he went straight out into the rain. It was only when he got to her doorstep that it had occurred to him that she might not be there.

But there she was, as he had somehow known she would be, looking very Bella in a short skirt and spectacular shoes, the golden hair falling around her face, and a glass in her hand.

'Come in,' she said in concern, stepping back and holding the door wide open. 'You're sodden!'

She helped him peel off his coat and hung it over the back of a chair in the kitchen. 'Sit down,' she said. 'I'll get you a drink. You look like you need it.'

He must look as shell-shocked as he felt, thought Josh as he dropped onto the old kitchen sofa, but he was feeling better already. There was something amazingly comforting about coming into this house, and especially this big, shabby kitchen with its mess and its clutter and its complete absence of steel or granite or anything remotely trendy.

'Here.' Bella put a glass of whisky into his hand and

sat cross-legged on the sofa, turning so that she could face him. 'Now, tell me what's happened.'

'Aisling's left me,' said Josh, a little surprised at how easy it was to say.

'Left you?' Bella stared at him blankly. 'What do you mean, *left* you?'

'She's gone. She doesn't want to marry me any more.'

It was almost a relief to see that the news was as unexpected to Bella as it had been to him. Josh would have felt a fool if he had been the last one to suspect anything, but looking at Bella he could see that she was as stunned as he had been.

'But...but...*why*?' She stammered. 'She was so excited the other day when we were all here. She couldn't talk about anything but marrying you.'

'She was trying to convince herself that was what she wanted,' he said evenly, 'but it wasn't. She's been in love with someone else all along.'

Bella shook her head trying to take it all in. 'Who is he? Do you know him?'

'His name's Bryn. I haven't had much to do with him but he's a senior executive at C.B.C. Aisling worked there before she joined us, and that's where she met him. She told me this evening that they'd had a passionate affair for nearly a year and that she was mad about him. But he's married, of course, and although he'd talked about leaving his wife, he kept coming up with excuses about how it wasn't the right time, and in the end Aisling decided to call the whole thing off.

'She was desperate to leave C.B.C. so that she wouldn't have to see him every day. I knew her because of previous work we had done for the company, so when I offered her a chance to move, she jumped at it. She told me tonight that it seemed as if it was meant.'

'No wonder she was so keen to come and work for you!' said Bella tartly. 'So all that stuff about wanting a more fulfilling job and working with a smaller organisation was her being just the teensiest bit economical with the truth, was it?'

'Not exactly. She enjoys working with us, but it wasn't quite the complete break she had hoped for,' said Josh. 'You know we're hoping to win this big contract from C.B.C.? If we get it, it'll be largely because of Aisling's contacts, and part of her job now is to deal with this Bryn on a regular basis, which hasn't been easy for her.'

Bella wasn't in the mood to feel sympathetic for Aisling's problems. 'God, Josh, you're starting to sound sorry for her!'

'I am a bit,' he said. 'Aisling tried everything she could to put him behind her, but she just couldn't. He's all she wants, and she had to try and cut herself off from that. That takes guts,' he added fairly.

'I might feel a bit more respect for her if she'd done it without using you,' said Bella. The blue eyes were stormy as she put her glass down on the table with a sharp click.

'That makes her sound too cynical.' It was ironic that he should be the one who ended up defending Aisling, Josh thought. 'It wasn't as if she didn't like me. She said she did, she liked me a lot, and she thought she could make a fresh start with me, but when it came down to it, it wasn't the same. She tried to talk herself into wanting to be with me, but it wasn't what she felt for Bryn. That was something much stronger and in the end she couldn't resist it.'

'And did she give *you* any thought in all of this?'

'I think she tried,' he said. 'She really wanted to make a go of it with me, and for a while it seemed as if it would work. She said she found me attractive, and we had lots of interests in common. There was no reason why it shouldn't really. Successful marriages have been built on less, and Aisling was hoping that if she threw herself into wedding preparations, she would forget all about Bryn.'

'So what made her change her mind?' Bella was still tight-lipped with anger on his behalf.

'Bryn rang her yesterday. He told her that he was getting a divorce and that he wanted to be with her. Aisling said that she knew then that it wouldn't be fair to get married to me feeling the way she still did about Bryn. She said she was sorry,' Josh added.

'Big of her!' said Bella tightly.

'Come on, Bella. At least she was honest,' he said. 'It was a classic relationship on the rebound. I'd much rather she told me now than after we were married. The longer she left telling me, the harder it would be.'

'I suppose so.'

Belatedly Bella realised that she wasn't being very supportive. 'I'm sorry,' she said, putting a hand on his arm. 'I just can't believe how calm you are. I can't believe any of it really. Aisling seemed so happy with you. And…and you were good together,' she added.

'Were we?' Josh drank his whisky. He was warmer and dryer, and sitting here on the sofa with Bella, it didn't seem so difficult to take in. 'It's hard to tell now.'

'I'm sorry, Josh,' she said again quietly and he shrugged and smiled crookedly.

'I'm sorry for dumping it all on you like this.'

'I seem to remember crying on your shoulder a few times,' said Bella, taking the empty glass from his hand and refilling it. She sat back down beside him straight-backed and crossed her legs once more.

'How do you feel?' she asked. 'I mean, really? No stiff upper lip!'

Josh sipped gratefully at his whisky. 'A bit stunned, I suppose.'

He couldn't tell Bella that his first reaction had shockingly been one of secret relief. He hadn't realised that he had had reservations at all until Aisling had announced that she didn't want to marry him after all, when he felt as if a burden he had hardly been aware of before had been lifted from his shoulders.

'It was the last thing I expected to hear when I got home this evening,' he told Bella. 'Aisling's been full of wedding plans all week, and we were working together all day. She seemed absolutely normal then. She's very good at keeping her professional and personal life separate.'

Bella didn't know about that. As far as she could see, Aisling had managed to sleep with her boss wherever she worked, and you couldn't mix up your personal and professional life more completely than that!

But she would have to be careful what she said. Josh was putting on a good front—stiff upper lip to the end— but Bella thought that he was more hurt than he was letting on. It was typical of him to take it on the chin like a gentleman and say that it was better for Aisling to break it all off now than later. No ranting and raving for Josh!

'What did you say?' she asked quietly instead.

'What could I say? If Aisling feels this away about Bryn, there's no point in her being with me.'

Bella ached for him. She had dreamt of hearing that Aisling wasn't going to marry Josh after all, but now that the moment had come, all she could think of was that he was hurting. Now was not the time to throw herself into his arms and tell him that she would love him for ever. He was raw and vulnerable, and still in love with Aisling, she reminded herself. He wasn't ready to think about anyone or anything else.

'Perhaps she'll come back,' Bella tried to comfort him. 'She might find that she doesn't feel quite the same when she's actually living with this Bryn. The romance wears off pretty quickly when you're picking up dirty socks and squabbling about who leaves the top off the toothpaste.'

'Perhaps,' said Josh, but he didn't sound convinced.

'Aisling's a fool if she doesn't,' Bella told him stoutly. 'She doesn't have any idea how lucky she is. She couldn't ask for more than you!'

'Except that she does,' he pointed out. 'I'm not the one she wants.'

Bella thought that her expression didn't change but Josh put his drink down abruptly and pulled her over to hug her. 'I'm sorry, Bella, I'm a fool. You know what that feels like.'

Agonisingly aware of his arms around her, she nodded into his shoulder. 'Yes,' she said quietly. 'I know what it's like.'

Everything should be perfect. He was free, she was free, and his arms were around her, holding her tight. What more could she want? Her face was pressed into his throat, and she could smell his skin. If she opened her eyes, she could see the pulse beating below his ear. It would be so easy to put her lips to it.

Except that it *wasn't* that easy, Bella realised. If she hadn't been able to tell him how she felt before because he was happy with Aisling, it was going to be even more difficult now. He might be putting a good face on it but Josh must be feeling raw with rejection. He needed her support, not the emotional equivalent of kicking a man when he was down.

It would be important for Josh that she at least was constant. He would need her to be the way she had always been. The last thing he wanted right now would be her

confusing the issue and throwing the basis of their friendship into question when the rest of his life was in flux.

What would be the point of telling him now, anyway?
Bella thought. Did she really want him turning to her on
the rebound, the way Aisling had done to him? No, she
would have to be very careful. Let him carry on believing
that it was Will she was breaking her heart for, at least for
the time being.

Josh's arms tightened around her. 'We're a pair, aren't
we?' he said, and his effort to sound jocular tightened
Bella's throat. 'Both in the reject bin! What's wrong with
us?'

'What's wrong with *them*?' Bella countered and Josh
kissed her hair.

'I'm glad you're here, Bella,' he said.

'I'm always here for you, Josh,' she said in a low voice,
knowing that he couldn't possibly understand how much
she meant it.

'I know,' he said quietly as he let her go.

Bella was trembling slightly as she sat back and picked
up her drink, and it was a real effort to keep her voice
steady. 'What are you going to do now?'

'There's nothing to do,' said Josh, reaching for his own
glass. 'Aisling and I are going to be working together, so
we'll just have to be civilised and carry on.'

'You mean she gets to keep her job after the way she's
treated you?' Bella was outraged.

'I can hardly sack her because she's not in love with
me,' Josh pointed out dryly. 'I don't think that would go
down very well at an industrial tribunal if she decided to
contest it! Anyway,' he said, 'she's very good at her job.
We need her if we want to clinch this big contract with
C.B.C.'

Bella couldn't believe that Aisling was *that* important.

'But it's going to be incredibly awkward, isn't it?' she objected. 'Everyone else at the office must know that you've been living together and were planning to get married.'

Josh shrugged. 'We'll just have to get on with it. I'll have a word with the others and ask them not to make things difficult for Aisling by asking too many questions. In any case, we'll be in the Seychelles next week, so they can get all the gossip out of the way then and with any luck they'll have something else to talk about when we get back.'

Bella eyed him with frustration. He could be infuriatingly reasonable at times! By rights, he should be swearing and tearing his hair out, and if not actually plotting revenge then at least vowing to make Aisling sorry.

But no! He was going to be the perfect gentleman and make everything nice and easy for her.

'Why don't you let Bryn take your place in the Seychelles while you're at it?' she said crossly. 'Pack their cases for them and take them to the airport!'

'I don't need to give up my place,' said Josh. 'Bryn's going anyway. He's one of C.B.C.'s most successful sales managers, and he's taking Aisling with him instead of his wife. He's changed the ticket into her name and has told whoever's doing all the organisation that Aisling will be taking his wife's place.'

Bella's jaw dropped. 'But…what about *you*?' she demanded.

'I'd be lying if I said I was looking forward to it,' he said with a sigh. 'Frankly, the last thing I feel like doing at the moment is spending a week stuck on an island having to suck up to potential clients. I'm no good at that kind of thing at the best of times. That's why it was important that Aisling came with me. She can do all the chit-chat.'

'If she's still working for you, she can manage that, can't she?' said Bella tightly.

Josh sighed and drank his whisky. 'I expect she will, but it won't be the same if she's not associated with me. If I'd been able to introduce my fiancée and keep everything on a very light social level, it would have made everything much easier. As it is, I'll stick out like a sore thumb being there on my own, and it's going to be very obvious that I'm there for work—the very impression C.B.C. didn't want me to give!'

'In that case, do you really need to go at all?'

'I think I'm going to have to,' said Josh, running a hand over his head in a gesture of weariness. 'C.B.C. have been insistent that they want me to be there to make personal contact with the executives I'd be working with, and the contract is too important to the company not to make that effort. It's not just about me. There are other people who work for me and who are depending on that contract for some security over the next three or four years. I'd be letting them down if I didn't go.'

He drained his glass and put it down on the table. 'I'll just have to do what I can. I'd better contact C.B.C. first thing tomorrow and let the know I won't be taking my fiancée with me after all. It'll be very short notice, but they might be able to cancel the flight and change my room.'

'Unless you just change the name of your fiancée,' said Bella.

Josh looked puzzled. 'What do you mean?'

'Well, Bryn seems to have been able to put his poor wife's ticket into Aisling's name. Why can't you do the same?'

'What would be the point of that? Aisling's got a ticket already.'

'I wasn't thinking of Aisling,' said Bella a little tartly. 'I was thinking of me.'

CHAPTER FIVE

HE STARED at her. 'You?' he said carefully.

'It sounds to me as if there's a spare ticket to the Seychelles going begging,' said Bella. 'You might not like the idea of a week on a tropical beach, but I haven't had a holiday for ages.'

She was groping her way cautiously, not wanting to spook Josh, but desperate to convince him to let her go with him. She couldn't bear the thought of him facing that week on his own. He would be fine, of course—Josh could cope with anything—but it would still be very hard for him to be there, having to face Aisling and Bryn every day. He might be tough, but even the tough needed some support occasionally.

'I could come with you,' she went on casually. 'I've been so miserable recently but I can't afford to go away by myself. I just thought that if there's a chance of spending a week on a beach at someone else's expense...' she trailed off suggestively, and Josh's mouth quirked.

'You could bear it?'

'I'd be helping you out at the same time,' Bella reassured him in a mock virtuous tone so that he wouldn't guess that was what she really wanted to do. 'You said yourself that it would be easier if you had a partner with you—who's to know that I'm not actually the fiancée you said you were taking with you?'

'Aisling and Bryn, for a start,' said Josh.

'I think after the way they've treated you, the least they could do is keep quiet,' said Bella stringently. 'None of the people you have to impress are going to know, are they? I might not have Aisling's contacts, but I can do chit-chat, as you call it, just as well as she can. Probably better,' she added, thinking about it.

'Oh, I know you can chit-chat for England!' said Josh.

'Well, then.'

He looked at her with a puzzled expression. 'I'm trying to think why it's not a good idea,' he said slowly. 'It feels like it shouldn't be, but I can't actually think of a reason why it wouldn't work.'

'It feels wrong because you'd be going with me instead of Aisling,' said Bella evenly. 'I know it's not what you wanted, Josh, but it *would* be a way to save face. It's not as if you'd have to be careful the way you would with a total stranger. We're so comfortable with each other I think we'd be quite convincing as a couple. You know how often we've been out and people have thought that we were together because of our body language.'

'I can see body language wouldn't be a problem,' Josh agreed, 'but other things might be. How comfortable would you be about sharing a room, which is what we'd have to do?'

'I could cope with that,' said Bella. 'It's not as if we've never done it before.'

'A long time ago,' he pointed out. 'That was when we were students. It's not the same any more, and it's no use pretending that it is.'

No, it wasn't the same, thought Bella, looking at him and remembering those carefree days when Josh had just been a mate, before he had started to seem as necessary to her as breathing.

'You're right,' she said slowly, 'it's not the same, but I just think it's going to be really hard for you to see Aisling with Bryn—which by the way is a totally stupid name. I bet you anything he's called Bryan and he's just dropped the "a"!'

She stopped, realising that she'd gone off at a tangent. 'Where was I?'

Josh grinned. 'You were trying to be deeply sympathetic about how hard it was going to be in the Seychelles and then you spoiled everything by making me laugh. I'm never going to be able to look at Bryn in the same way again!'

'Oh, yes,' said Bella, delighted to see the glint back in Josh's eyes but refusing to let herself be sidetracked onto the issue of Bryn's name again. 'Well, I do think it will be incredibly difficult and I can't help feeling that it would be easier if you had a friend with you. Don't you think so?' she asked anxiously, suddenly afraid that she was pushing him into something that he didn't want to do.

'I suppose that depends on the friend,' said Josh, straight-faced, and then relented. 'But yes, if you mean you, it would be nice—very nice!—to have some support.'

'That's what I'd be there for,' Bella told him. 'And if supporting you means pretending to be your fiancée to keep up appearances, fine, and if *that* means sharing a room, I'm not exactly going to make a fuss. We know each other too well for that.'

'What if it means sharing a bed?'

Bella hesitated, picking her words with care. 'We both know how things are, Josh,' she said. 'I know you're in love with Aisling, you know about Will. There's not much room for misunderstanding in our case, is there?'

She reached for his empty glass. 'Have a think about it while I get you another drink.'

Josh had already had two stiff whiskies. Perhaps that was why Bella's idea was seeming to make perfect sense, he thought hazily. But she was right, wasn't she? How could it be awkward for two such old friends to share a bed? Especially when it was absolutely clear that she was still in love with Will? There would be no room for any misunderstanding *there*, just as she had said.

And as for him, thought Josh, he was naturally devastated about Aisling. No man with any sense of decency would be sitting there, barely hours after his engagement had been broken off, wondering what it would be like to share a bed with another woman.

He wouldn't be thinking about her softness as she hugged him—purely sympathetically, of course—or the fragrance of her hair. About the indignation in her blue eyes or the curve of her mouth as she smiled.

He certainly wouldn't be thinking that sleeping with her might not be that easy after all.

Discovering that you weren't the decent man you thought you were was all he needed after the day he had had, thought Josh with an inward sigh.

Really, he didn't deserve Bella's sympathy, Josh thought guiltily. He knew she was offering to go out to the Seychelles because she felt sorry for him, but she probably *could* do with a break. She had had a hard time over Will, and if her finances were as chaotic as usual, he could well believe that she couldn't afford a holiday by herself.

Giving Bella a week in the sun would at least be one good thing to come out of this whole sorry mess with Aisling. Josh didn't mind letting her believe that he needed her support more than in fact he did. And it would be good to have her there, he had to admit. She would charm everyone, with the possible exception of Aisling and Bryn, and her presence would make things less awkward all round.

Oh, yes, there were lots of reasons why it would be good to take Bella up on her offer, but when it came down to it, the only one that mattered was that he wanted her with him. Josh had had enough intensity and conversations about weddings over the last few weeks. It would be fun with Bella.

Here she was, putting another enormous whisky into his hand. 'Well?' she asked, 'Have you had a think?'

'I have.'

'And?'

'And I think we should go for it,' he said, and smiled at Bella's whoop of delight before reminding himself that he would need to be careful. If he slipped too quickly out of the role of rejected fiancé, she might start to wonder why he needed her there at all. 'I think it would make things easier for Aisling too,' he said.

The blue eyes narrowed. 'That was naturally my main concern!'

'Sarcasm, Bella?'

'Just another service we offer!' she retorted even more sarcastically. 'Honestly, Josh, the woman only dumped you a couple of hours ago! I know how important she is to you, but I think it's a bit early for you to be bending over backwards to *make things easier* for her! What about a bit of anger or bitterness? I'm sure it would be much more healthy!'

'The thing is, I can't feel that way about Aisling,' said Josh, knowing that it was a lack in himself. If he had really loved Aisling, he would have been just as bitter and angry as Bella wanted him to be. As it was, he had been much angrier with Will for hurting Bella. 'You weren't angry or bitter about Will,' he pointed out, 'but I can tell that you're heartbroken all the same.'

Bella opened her mouth, only to change her mind about what she was going to say and close it again. 'I hope you aren't expecting me to be nice to Aisling too?' she said after a moment, and Josh wondered what she had meant to say instead. 'I'm not as tolerant as you.'

'I'd rather you were,' he told her. 'It's not going to be an easy time for any of us, but we need to focus on getting the C.B.C. contract. Given that we're supposed to be teaching these guys how to communicate effectively and work as a team, it's not going to impress them if we're all squabbling amongst ourselves.'

'Oh, all right,' sighed Bella with a martyred air. 'I'll be good.'

Josh smiled and sipped at his whisky as he settled back into the sofa, stretching his legs out in front of him. For a man who was supposed to have had his heart broken earlier that evening he was feeling surprisingly mellow. It was good to be back on his own with Bella again. It hadn't been same when Aisling had been around.

'So that's settled then.' Bella took up her familiar position on the sofa beside him, with crossed legs and a straight back. 'When do we leave?'

'Check-in is noon on Monday,' he told her. 'I'll come and pick you up in the morning and we can go out to Heathrow together.'

Bella flashed him a look underneath her lashes. 'You mean you don't trust me not to be late!'

'I know that if it was up to you you'd stroll up five minutes before the plane's due to leave,' said Josh, 'but I don't think my nerves will stand it! Since we're pretending to be engaged, why don't you go the whole hog and pretend to be a normal person who turns up on time for a change?'

Bella poked her tongue at him. She had never actually missed a plane, had she? True, there had been a couple of close calls, and she had given up booking train tickets in advance, but really, it wasn't as if planes ever left on time anyway.

'I suppose you'll be wanting to leave at the crack of dawn on Monday and get there four hours early just to be on the safe side,' she grumbled. 'It doesn't leave long to get ready. Still, I suppose I don't need much.'

Mentally, Bella ran an eye over her wardrobe. It had been so long since she had had a decent holiday all her hot-weather clothes were hopelessly out of date. She might just have to have a little shop tomorrow. Josh wouldn't understand, but facing Aisling required a major style offensive. Nothing too obvious, of course, but certainly enough to make Aisling feel that she was never *quite* wearing the right thing...

Josh was evidently thinking along more practical lines.

'What about your job, Bella? Will they let you take time off at such short notice?'

Why was Josh worrying about her job? There were far more essential things to think about. Reluctantly, Bella dragged her attention away from the important question of a wardrobe designed with the daily discomfiture of Aisling in mind.

'I might try ringing my boss at home later,' she said. 'She won't like it, but we're not that busy at the moment and I've done lots of overtime recently so I'm entitled to time off in lieu. Luckily, Louise is a real romantic,' she confided. 'If she gets too sticky about the whole thing I'll just tell her we've decided to get married on the spur of the moment and that you're whisking me off to the Seychelles to celebrate.'

Josh looked unconvinced. 'Don't tell her that we've known each other for fourteen years,' he said. 'It would take more than a confirmed romantic to interpret that as a whirlwind affair!'

'Oh, I don't know,' said Bella, considering the matter. 'Louise knows we've been friends a long time, but I'll just tell her that everything has suddenly changed and that realising that we were meant to be more than friends has caught us both unawares.'

There was a tiny pause. 'Do you think she's likely to fall for that?' said Josh in a dry voice.

'It happens,' she said without looking at him. 'Sometimes you fall in love when you least expect it.'

'It sounds quite convincing when you put it like that,' he said.

Another silence. For some reason Bella's heart was slamming against her ribs. Don't look at him, she told herself frantically. You'll only make a fool of yourself.

Her eyes skittered around the room but it was as if an invisible, irresistible force was dragging them back to Josh's face, where their gazes locked for a long moment before Bella managed to wrench hers away.

'As long as it convinces Louise,' she said shakily. 'That's the main thing.'

'Of course,' echoed Josh. 'That's the main thing.'

In spite of her best efforts, Bella found her eyes flickering back to his once more before they both looked away.

The pause was even longer this time, and it reverberated unnervingly up and down Bella's spine. She longed to be able to say something to break the silence but her mind had gone blank and all she could think of was how close Josh was and how easy it would be to lean over and touch him.

She swirled her glass, staring down into it as if fascinated, but she was so acutely aware of Josh by that stage that she might as well have been staring straight at him. It was as if those fleeting eye contacts had imprinted an unnervingly vivid image of him on her brain, not of the old familiar Josh, but of a stranger, a man, with a cool mouth and a firm jaw and intriguing creases around his eyes.

In the end it was Josh who spoke first. He cleared his throat. 'Are you sure you're happy to do this, Bella?' he asked awkwardly, as if he too was unsettled by the strange tightening of the atmosphere.

Flippancy was the only response Bella was capable of right then. 'Well, a free week in the Seychelles *will* be a bit of bore, of course, but for you…anything!'

'It's just that you didn't sound too keen on the idea when Aisling was talking about it.'

'That's because she kept going on about all the activities you would be doing together. I presume all the hearty stuff isn't compulsory.' Belatedly a wary look crept into the blue eyes. 'I don't have to go diving, do I?'

Josh shook his head. 'You would if you loved me,' he said solemnly. 'If you want to convince people that you're my fiancée, you probably should make an effort to get involved in some the activities.'

His face was completely straight, but she caught the gleam of humour in his eyes. He was teasing…phew!

'I'll just tell everybody that our relationship is based on the attraction of opposites,' she said firmly. 'Bet you anything I won't be the only person heading straight for the beach, so if it's all the same to you, I'll concentrate my charm offensive there. After a few days on a lounger, with nothing to do but listen to the coconuts drop or cool off with a paddle in the Indian Ocean I should be able to be nice to anybody—even Aisling!'

'You're going *where*?' said Kate when Bella rang her the next morning. 'With *who*?'

Impatiently, Bella explained the situation all over again. She had already been through all this with Phoebe. Now that she was used to the idea herself, it seemed such an obvious solution that she couldn't understand why the others didn't seem to grasp it at once.

'So let me get this right,' said Kate at last. 'You and Josh have got engaged without even *consulting* me or Phoebe?'

'It's just for a week,' said Bella. 'And it's just pretending. I don't know why you're making such a big deal of it,' she huffed. 'You and Finn did exactly the same thing.'

'Yes, and look what happened!' said Kate. 'I'm all for it, but you want to be careful, Bella. Pretending isn't nearly as easy as you think in that situation.'

'I know,' said Bella, whose main problem wasn't going to be pretending that she was in love with Josh but pretending that she wasn't.

Kate hesitated. 'It will be difficult for Josh, too. He must be feeling pretty raw about Aisling and it's going to be awful for him having to see her with this other guy so soon. You can't expect even someone as level-headed as Josh to be thinking clearly under those circumstances.'

'What are you trying to say, Kate?'

'Just…be careful,' she said slowly. 'I know you and Josh are old friends, but you're going to be thrown into a very intimate situation and things won't be the same. It's easy to imagine how you might end up turning to each other.'

'I thought you and Phoebe wanted us to end up together?' said Bella, trying to make a joke of it, but Kate took her seriously.

'Only if it's for the right reasons. Josh deserves better than getting together because you feel restless and unsettled, and you deserve more than being second-best to Aisling.'

Bella was still thinking of this conversation when she

met Josh for lunch later that day so that he could report that he had been able to change Aisling's ticket into Bella's name, and Bella that after much grumbling her boss had agreed to her having the whole week off.

Kate was right, she knew that, and she *would* be careful, Bella vowed, but her spirits had risen in spite of herself at the prospect of the week ahead.

She felt better today, less edgy and aware. It was like old times, meeting Josh for lunch on a Saturday, and they were both more relaxed, talking and laughing as if the tension of the night before had never happened.

So much so, in fact, that Bella had to keep reminding herself about Aisling. Josh seemed to be fine, but then, he would. The phrase 'keeping a stiff upper lip' might have been coined especially for him.

Josh hadn't forgotten about Aisling though. 'I rang her this morning,' he told Bella.

'What was that like?' she asked with a grimace, imagining what a tense conversation it must have been. 'Was it awful?'

'No, it was fine.' Josh had been surprised himself at how normal it had all seemed. 'I told her that you were going in her place and she and Bryn have promised not to let on to anyone else that you and I aren't really a couple.'

Big of her, thought Bella with a mental sniff.

'If they don't say anything, it shouldn't be a problem to convince the others,' Josh went on. 'All you need is a ring to flash around and no one will think to question whether you're a real fiancée or not.'

Bella looked down at her fingers. She had a silver ring on her right hand but it wasn't the kind of thing you could really pass off as an engagement ring. What she needed was a rock. Glass would do, she thought. She could never tell the difference between real gems and glass, and she bet none of the others would be able to either.

Mentally she reviewed her jewellery. She had plenty of fun earrings and necklaces but very few rings. 'I'm not sure I've got anything suitable,' she said doubtfully.

'I'll buy you one,' said Josh. Glancing at his watch, he drained his glass and pushed back his chair. 'Come on, let's go and do it now.'

'You can't buy me a ring!'

'Why not?'

'Well…it doesn't seem right,' said Bella, getting to her feet more slowly and shrugging on her coat. 'Anyway, there's no need surely,' she added, thinking about the knuckleduster Aisling had been flaunting at the engagement dinner. 'What about the ring you bought Aisling?'

'I said she could keep it.'

'And she did?' asked Bella indignantly.

Josh was in one of his infuriatingly reasonable moods. 'What was I going to do with it?' he pointed out.

'You could have taken it back to the shop!'

He held open the door of the bar for her. 'I think that would have been a bit petty, don't you?'

'No, I don't!' Bella shivered as they emerged into the raw November afternoon. Suddenly the Seychelles seemed very, very appealing. 'I can't believe Aisling could coolly walk off with that ring after the way she treated you! It must have cost you a fortune. Really, you're too much of a gentleman for your own good sometimes, Josh!' she told him, turning up her collar against the wind.

'I think having the ring flung back in my face would have been worse,' said Josh. 'Besides, Aisling loved that ring. If she wanted to keep something from me, I didn't mind.'

She must shut up about Aisling, Bella caught herself up

guiltily, remembering what Kate had said. Just because Josh was putting on a good face didn't mean he wasn't hurting inside, and the ring would be a sensitive issue. He could be hoping that Aisling would decide to come back when she realised that generous men who let you kick them in the teeth and walk away with a ring worth thousands of pounds were few and far between.

'It just seems a waste of money to buy another ring for me,' she said in an attempt to steer the subject away from Aisling.

'We're not paying for anything else during this week,' Josh pointed out. 'C.B.C. are even covering the bar bills, so I can look on it as a justifiable expense. If it makes a difference to winning that contract, it might even be tax deductible! Look, that's where we bought Aisling's ring,' he said suddenly, dragging a still reluctant Bella over the road.

'We can't go in there,' she protested, eying the discreet display of jewellery in the window. There were no prices on view, always a bad sign. The whole place looked very classy.

And very expensive.

Josh didn't appear to be at all intimidated. 'Why not?'

'They might remember you buying that ring for Aisling, for a start.'

'Nonsense,' he said briskly, propelling her towards the door. 'Come on, Bella. They must have loads of customers and it's over a month since Aisling and I were here. There's no way they're going to remember me.'

'Good afternoon, sir,' said the urbane man behind the counter. 'How nice to see you again. What can we do for you today?'

'See!' hissed Bella, turning back towards the door, but Josh had her arm in a firm grip and was forcing her on.

He didn't even have the grace to look embarrassed, (a) at being recognised, and (b) at being proved so comprehensively wrong!

'We'd like to look at your engagement rings, please,' he said coolly.

The jeweller took his request without a blink. 'Certainly, sir. Did you have anything in particular in mind? Diamonds, perhaps? Or emeralds?'

'Not emeralds,' said Josh, appreciating the sly reference to the ring he had bought Aisling. 'We had emeralds last time.' He smiled blandly, not at all discomfited by any other subtle digs the jeweller might have up his sleeve.

'This lady is very different,' he said, drawing forward a fierily blushing Bella. 'Have you got any nice sapphires?'

'He must be wondering what on earth you're up to,' she whispered as the jeweller went in search of sapphires and kept his inevitable reflections to himself.

'Let him wonder,' said Josh. 'It's not his business how many rings I buy or who I buy them for. If he thinks I'll be coming back on a regular basis, he might even offer me a discount for regular custom!'

When the tray was laid reverently before her, Bella was dazzled by the array of beautiful rings. She wished there were prices on so that she could at least choose the cheapest.

'Don't pick out the smallest,' said Josh, reading her mind. 'It'll just make me look mean. Choose one you really like.'

'I don't know…' Bella dithered over the tray until he selected an exquisite sapphire with diamonds clustered around it.

'Here, try this one,' he said and held out his hand in a way that made it impossible for Bella to do anything other than put hers into it.

Excruciatingly aware of the warmth and strength of his fingers, and paralysed by a new and sudden shyness, Bella stared fixedly at the ring.

'Do you like it?' asked Josh, who seemed to have forgotten that he was still holding her hand.

'It's lovely.' She swallowed and drew her hand free. 'I'm sure all these are far too expensive, though,' she whispered.

'Look, Bella, will you stop worrying about the expense,' said Josh, exasperated. If he had noticed her not-so-subtle attempt to free her hand, he gave no sign of it. 'You can give it back at the end of week and I'll sell it back if that makes you feel any better.'

It wouldn't, but she could hardly say so. 'I suppose so,' said Bella instead.

'Right. Now, relax and enjoy it.' He picked out another ring. 'What about this one?'

Eventually they chose a very simple band of square-cut sapphires and diamonds which fitted her finger perfectly. Bella admired it glinting on her hand. She had never worn anything like it before. It was going to make the rest of her jewellery look cheap and tatty, but now that she had it on her finger she wasn't sure how she was ever going to be able to bear taking it off.

She would worry about that later, Bella decided, her earlier doubts and hesitations dissolved in the pleasure of the sparkling stones. Nothing had changed. It was still too early to let Josh know how she felt, and much too soon to assume that he was over Aisling, no matter how together he seemed, but at least he was free now. At least she could hope. For now she had Josh beside her and a whole week with him to look forward to.

And his ring on her finger.

Bella's spirits soared and she smiled as Josh came back

from a discreet exchange with the jeweller. 'It's beautiful,' she told him. She had no idea how much he had paid, but it certainly hadn't been cheap, 'I'll look after it,' she promised before he had a chance to tell her not to lose it.

'Please do,' he said with a crooked smile.

Ah, definitely *not* cheap then.

Over his shoulder, Bella could see the jeweller watching them with a speculative expression. What was he thinking? Had he guessed that Aisling had dumped Josh, and that she was a mere substitute?

They couldn't have that, thought Bella. If he had to think anything, it was that Josh was the kind of man who had women queuing up to marry him, and preferably the sort of cad who could string two, and possibly more, along at the same time.

Bella glanced at Josh, so obviously decent and straightforward and reliable. Still, the jeweller wasn't to know that his restrained appearance didn't disguise a bounder of the first order, was he? It would be fun to make him believe that here was a case of still waters running deep!

'Thank you, darling,' she said and to Josh's evident surprise, fortunately concealed from the jeweller, she put her arms around his neck and smiled seductively at him. 'I'll thank you properly when we get home,' she said throatily, 'so this is just to be going on with…'

To the extent that Bella had a ''plan'', it was to kiss Josh on the corner of his mouth, but now that she actually had her arms around his neck and an excuse, however frivolous, that *did* seem a waste of an opportunity. If she wanted the jeweller to secretly admire and envy Josh, a peck on the cheek simply wasn't enough.

In any case, it seemed as if her lips had a plan of their own. They skimmed the crease of his cheek, drawn by some irresistible force to his mouth where they settled as if they had found the one place they were meant to be, and the next thing Bella knew she was kissing Josh in a way she had never kissed him before and it didn't feel particularly daring or strange at all. It felt utterly and completely right.

She felt Josh's arm encircle her waist and draw her closer. After the first stunned moment, he had evidently decided to go with the flow and ask questions later. The trouble was that having started the kiss, Bella didn't know how to end it.

Worse, she didn't want to.

With a superhuman effort, she managed to withdraw her lips for a fraction of a second before succumbing to the desire for just one kiss more, and the next time she tried, it was Josh who followed her mouth with his and refused to let her break contact.

It was as if their kisses had taken on a will of their own, as the initial sweetness and rightness gathered and hardened into something much more dangerous, something almost scary that clutched at the base of Bella's spine. Josh must have felt the same frisson, for he was the one who succeeded at last in lifting his head.

They stared at each other for a long, shaken moment before Josh swallowed hard and collected himself with an effort. 'I think we'd better go,' he said.

He turned to thank the jeweller who was studiously rearranging the rings on the tray, a suspicion of a smile hovering about his mouth, while Bella struggled to get herself under control. She had always thought the phrase 'weak at the knees' a complete cliché, but suddenly she knew exactly what it meant. It wasn't just her knees, either. Her whole body felt disjointed and she wondered how she was going to get out of the door without support.

She had visions of herself groping her way around the counters, but in the end Josh simply took her arm and propelled her through the door. Once safely outside though, he let her go abruptly.

CHAPTER SIX

'DO YOU want to tell me what that was all about?' he asked, and Bella noted with some resentment that he had his breathing well under control once more.

Which was more than could be said for her.

'I was just trying to bolster your image,' she said, but her voice came out all thin and funny and breathy at all the wrong points.

She told Josh her plan to impress the jeweller, but it sounded even stupider when punctuated by odd gasps for breath, and when she finally stumbled to the end she wasn't surprised to see Josh shake his head in exasperated disbelief.

'I don't want you to think I don't appreciate the thought,' he said dryly, 'but I'd already told him the truth.'

Nothing could have been guaranteed to cure Bella's breathing problems more quickly. 'You did *what*?' she demanded. 'Why?'

'I could tell he was wondering what was going on, and I didn't want him thinking that I was taking advantage of you.'

It was Bella's turn to be exasperated. 'That's absolutely typical of you, Josh! I go to all that effort to improve your image with people and you just throw the opportunity away!' She scowled, remembering the jeweller's smile as he opened the door for her. 'He must have thought I was a complete idiot kissing you like that!'

Josh started to grin. 'I must be his favourite customer

now. Not only do I buy extremely expensive rings from him, but he gets free entertainment thrown in!'

How humiliating! Bella tried to be offended, but after a moment she gave in and laughed too. Perhaps it was just as well to treat the whole incident as a joke. It felt so good to be laughing with Josh again, relaxing the tension between them after that shattering kiss.

She would have to be careful, Bella decided as Josh spotted the bus they wanted, and they ran for the stop. She had probably revealed far more of herself in that kiss than she had intended.

The last thing she wanted was for Josh to think that she was trying to worm her way into Aisling's place. That would make her seem like an emotional ambulance-chaser, one of those girls who cruised around looking for relationships in trouble before homing in on the newly single man.

Bella had known several girls who complained that the lack of men meant that unless they moved quickly, they would never get a man at all, but she didn't want Josh thinking that she was like them. She didn't want him turning to her for comfort, or falling into bed with her just because she was there and available and it would be easy.

No, thought Bella, that wouldn't be enough. She wanted to be the beat of his heart. She wanted him to love her and want her and need her, to feel that she was the only one who could make his life complete. To recognise, as she had done, that what he had been looking for had been right in front of him all along.

But Josh needed to realise that for himself. In the meantime, she would have to be very patient.

And, yes, careful, just as Kate had warned.

'You do realise that we're only going for a week?' said Josh when he saw the size of Bella's suitcase on Monday morning.

Bella looked at the neat cabin bag at his feet. 'Do *you* realise that we're going for more than five minutes?'

'Now, now, children, don't quarrel,' said Phoebe, banging the door of the boot closed. She had offered to drop them off at the airport on her way down to Devon to interview a woman who claimed that cats had a language which she could understand.

'Which should be fun,' Phoebe had said, 'but not as much fun as a week in the Seychelles!'

She kissed Josh and gave Bella an extra tight hug. 'Have a lovely time, both of you,' she said. 'We're all hoping that you two are going to follow tradition and that your mock engagement will turn into a real one as well. Then we can give you a party when you come home!'

'No fear of that,' said Josh lightly. He nodded at his neat little bag sitting next to Bella's huge case. 'You only need to look at how much we think is essential for a week away to see that we're totally incompatible!'

'There's more to love than luggage, Josh,' said Phoebe with a wink at Bella, who was looking daggers at her over her heavy hints.

Ignoring her friend's pointed glare, Phoebe blew them a kiss, got into the car and drove off smartly, leaving Josh and Bella with their mismatching baggage standing in front of the terminal.

'I suppose we're going to get a lot of that,' said Josh carefully.

'I'm afraid so,' Bella sighed. 'I should never have told Kate and Phoebe that I was going with you instead of Aisling. Now they're determined that we're going to end up married the way they did.'

A raw November wind was blowing her hair about her face, and she held it back with her hand as she glanced at him. 'It's ridiculous, of course, and I've told them there's no question of it, but you know what they're like. That's why I'm glad you said what you did about being incompatible,' she added casually.

'It didn't seem to have much effect on Phoebe,' Josh pointed out with a wry look.

'No, well, they'll realise what a stupid idea it is when we come home in a week's time and go right back to the way we were before.'

'Right,' said Josh.

The only trouble was, he couldn't remember how things had been before Bella had kissed him on Saturday. How was he going to remember what they were like after a week sleeping next to her?

The thought of it made something twist deep inside Josh. He wished Bella hadn't kissed him.

He hadn't been prepared for that jolt of response when her lips touched his, and although he knew he should be taking it lightly, still he had found himself holding her against him, tightening his arm, refusing to let her break the kiss. Josh could still feel how warm and pliant she had been. He couldn't get her softness or the sweetness of her lips or the deep, dark thrill that had uncoiled so unexpectedly out of his mind.

He would have to try, Josh told himself sternly. Bella had laughed afterwards, and it had been clear that she didn't intend to take the kiss seriously at all, so he should do the same. After all, this was Bella, not some mysteriously sexy and seductive stranger.

He glanced at her now, hugging her arms against the cold while the long, golden hair was whipped about her face. Yes, that was Bella all right. She was as stylish as ever, but quite unsuitably dressed for travel in a short fig-ure-hugging dress that looked as if would crease the moment she sat down. All she had to keep her warm was an insubstantial little cardigan, and her feet with their immaculately painted toes were encased in fragile sandals with—Josh did a double take—yes, *jewelled* straps of all things. Over the years, Bella's ridiculously impractical shoes had become something of a running joke, but these ones really took the biscuit!

Aisling would never get on a plane wearing shoes like that, even without all those absurd fake jewels. Once her feet had swollen during the long flight, there wasn't a hope in hell that Bella would be able to get those tiny straps on again, so she would be hobbling off the plane at best.

No doubt Bella would carry it off with style, though. She might be unsuitably dressed but she was undeniably gorgeous with her long legs, that warm curving mouth and those blue eyes with their tilting lashes.

Josh made himself look away. She had always been gorgeous, of course. He just wished that he could stop noticing just how gorgeous now. There was no point in noticing. Bella was his friend, and any relationship they had was based on personality and not on looks.

'We both know how things are,' she had said. *'I know you're in love with Aisling, and you know about Will.'* There would be no room for misunderstanding, she had said.

And there wouldn't be, Josh told himself firmly.

'Come on,' he said, seeing her shiver, 'let's go and check in.' He reached for her case only to grunt as he heaved it off the ground. 'For God's sake, Bella! What have you got in here?'

'Just a few essentials,' she said airily.

'But you're only going to lie on a beach! How many clothes can you wear every day?'

'It's not just clothes,' Bella said, teetering along beside him in her absurd shoes. 'You've got to be very careful about the sun nowadays. UV rays can do terrible things to your skin and hair, so I've brought all sorts of special moisturisers and sun screen and after-sun lotions. And then you've got to worry about your hair,' she told Josh, who had never given his hair a moment's thought. 'I've got a protective lotion to put on when I go into the sea, and a conditioner for when I come out, and there's shampoo, of course, and another conditioner for the evening…'

She chattered on as they waited in the queue for the check-in desk. Josh was desperately aware of her beside him as she combed out the tangles in her wind-blown hair and threw the golden mass back from her face. She was like a cat with her constant grooming, he tried to think disapprovingly, but he kept losing track of what she was saying and why he was supposed to be exasperated as his mind drifted back to the warmth and softness of her lips against his.

'Anyway, enough of that.' Bella shook back her hair and laid a hand on his arm, her eyes deep and very blue. 'How are you feeling, Josh?'

How *was* he feeling?

Alarmed by the frisson that went through him at the touch of her hand.

Disturbed by the memories of her kiss.

Guilty about the treacherous way his mind kept wandering.

'Fine,' said Josh a little hoarsely.

'Yes, I know you're going to *say* fine,' she said as the queue shuffled forwards, 'but you don't need to be stiff-upper-lipped with me. How do you really feel? Are you dreading seeing Aisling with Bryan or Bryn or whatever he calls himself?'

Aisling. Josh clutched at the thought of her. She was the perfect excuse for his distraction this morning.

'I can't say I'm looking forward to it,' he said.

She tucked a hand into his, and when he looked at her, the blue eyes were warm with sympathy. 'I know it will be hard,' she said, 'but don't forget that I'm here for you.'

Josh's throat was absurdly tight. 'Thanks, Bella,' he managed and his fingers curled and tightened around hers in spite of himself. 'You're a good friend.'

'I always will be,' said Bella, her own smile wavering a little.

All in all, it was a relief when they reached the check-in desk at last, and Josh was forced to let go of her hand. He had a nasty feeling that he wouldn't have been able to do it otherwise.

He must pull himself together, he told himself with an edge of desperation. Wasn't he supposed to be the expert on dealing with difficult situations? The trouble was that it was easy to know what to do when you had to rescue a colleague who had fallen down a crevasse in the ice, or get someone dangerously ill out of the jungle and into hospital when your radio wasn't working and it was three days' trek to the nearest settlement.

Even winning the contract with C.B.C. was a doddle compared to coping with this sudden, disturbing awareness of his best friend. Josh didn't like feeling out of control. He could train executives how to analyse a situation, assess the risks involved and communicate effectively to resolve problems, but he didn't know how to deal with this.

He handed Bella her boarding pass. 'We'd better go and find the others,' he said, clearing his throat. 'They're probably in the bar.'

It was Bella who spotted Aisling first, warning Josh with a nudge as she put her arm through his and tilted her chin at a combative angle. There was a look in her eyes that Josh recognised, and it usually meant trouble. When Bella wore that expression it made you very glad that she was on your side.

'You promised you would be nice,' he reminded her. 'Remember we've got a contract to win here.'

'Of course,' said Bella, but Josh didn't entirely trust the smile she flashed at him.

He was so preoccupied with whether she would behave that he came face to face with Aisling before he had a chance to think about how it was going to feel to confront the woman he had been planning to marry until three days ago. In the event, Josh was puzzled to find that he didn't feel anything at all.

'Hello,' he said, as he kissed her on the cheek. 'You're looking very well.'

It was true. He had never seen her look so beautiful before. She was glowing with happiness. If Josh had needed anything to convince him that Aisling had made the right decision, one look at her now would have been enough. He had never made her happy the way being with Bryn clearly did.

As he had guessed, she was dressed much more sensibly than Bella in loose khaki trousers, a soft cream shirt and sandals that managed to look elegant and practical at the same time.

'Hi, Josh,' she greeted him, and then lowered her voice so that none of the others waiting in the bar with them would hear. 'How *are* you?'

Josh was beginning to get a little tired of being asked that. 'I'm fine,' he said again, although he doubted whether Aisling would believe him any more than Bella had. He *was* fine, though. Why couldn't they just accept that?

Beside him he could feel Bella bristling but she seemed

to have herself under control. 'You remember Bella, don't you?'

'Hello, Aisling,' she said in a frosty voice.

There was scarcely more warmth in the way Aisling returned her greeting, and the green eyes were distinctly cool.

'Congratulations,' she said for the benefit of their audience. 'I gather you and Josh have just got engaged,' she added. 'Quite a whirlwind romance!'

'No,' said Bella, meeting her eyes squarely. 'It's just taken us fourteen years to realise how much we love each other.'

'Convenient that you realised in time for a trip to the Seychelles,' Aisling commented slyly.

Josh tensed, but Bella managed an insincere smile. 'Wasn't it?' she said sweetly. 'I can't tell you how thrilled I am.'

She turned to the man beside Aisling. He was tall and classically good-looking and seemed exceptionally pleased with himself, Josh noted sourly. Just Bella's type, in fact. He found himself watching her anxiously, but she just shook Bryn's hand with a cool smile.

'I bet you anything I'm right about him being called Bryan,' she whispered under her breath to Josh as he steered her quickly away to meet some of the others. 'See if you can get a look at his passport!'

'You're supposed to be being good,' said Josh repressively, but he couldn't help grinning.

As if by common consent the party had all forgathered in the bar. There were sixteen of them altogether, and although those who worked for C.B.C. naturally knew each other, their partners were strangers and conversation had evidently been stilted to begin with.

Things picked up noticeably when Bella joined the

group. She had always had an ability to get the party go-ing, and before long she was making everyone laugh and relax. Josh watched her animated face as she leant forward to draw out the shy wife of one of the junior C.B.C. ex-ecutives. She might not have the necessary skills to survive out in the wild, but there was nothing he or anyone else could tell her about how to get on in a social setting!

He had found them seats on the other side of the group from Aisling and Bryn, who were talking to the senior C.B.C. manager and her partner, and he began to relax himself until he noticed that Bella had sat back next to him and was sending searching glances at Bryn from be-neath her lashes.

Josh's immediate thought was that she had found Bryn attractive after all, and he glowered. 'Why do you keep staring at Bryn?' he demanded crossly.

Bella leant closer. 'I'm trying to imagine him with a personality,' she confided in his ear and Josh was startled at the rush of relief he felt.

'He's completely bland,' she went on, going back to her study of Bryn with a puzzled frown. 'I can't understand it. How could Aisling leave you for someone like that?'

'She's in love with him,' said Josh, trying to be fair.

'Yes, that's obvious,' Bella agreed. 'She's all lit up, and anyone can see that it's because of him. I just can't see *why*, that's all.'

Josh followed her gaze. Now that he knew that Bella wasn't interested, he could study the other man dispas-sionately. 'He's very good-looking,' he offered as an ex-planation.

'I suppose so.' Bella sounded unconvinced, and Josh glanced at her in some surprise.

'I'd have said that he was just your type.'

She looked taken aback. 'Really?'

'He's got that smug, self-satisfied look you seem to go for,' said Josh, unable to resist it. 'You've got to admit that he looks a bit like Will, who looked just like all your other boyfriends.'

Bella stared openly at Bryn. 'I don't think he looks *anything* like Will,' she told him. 'There's nothing to him at all.'

Josh didn't think there had been anything to Will, either, but he remembered just in time that Bella was in love with the man. He would have to be more tactful. *She* hadn't stooped to making personal comments about Aisling, although knowing the sharpness of her tongue on occasion and judging by the frostiness of the atmosphere between the two women she was more than capable of it.

'Bryn's not your type, then?' he asked lightly instead, and she turned from Bryn to look directly at him, blue eyes unusually serious.

'No,' she said. 'He's not my type at all.'

Josh was conscious of an odd hollow feeling inside as he stared back into her eyes, and he swallowed. 'Good,' he said, but his voice sounded very strange.

He felt a bit odd too. If he wasn't someone who was never ill, he would be wondering if he was coming down with something. At least it would explain this peculiar fuzzy feeling and inability to focus. He shook his head slightly, hoping to clear it. He must be more tired than he had thought.

Bella had turned and introduced herself to the woman sitting on her other side.

'I've been admiring your ring,' Bella's new friend was saying. When Josh looked at her more closely he realised that he had met her before. What was her name again? Sue? Sarah? No, Sally, he remembered.

'It's beautiful,' Sally said enviously. 'Have you two been engaged long?'

'Not long, no,' said Bella. 'Actually, only since last Friday.'

'Oh, how romantic!'

'Well, it is and it isn't,' Bella said. 'We've known each other for a long time, so it's not as if we're rushing into anything.'

'So what made you decide to get married now?'

Bella glanced at Josh and then away. 'It's a funny thing,' she said slowly. 'I just looked at him one day and knew that I wanted to spend the rest of my life with him, and that being friends wasn't enough any more.'

Sally smiled. 'And Josh felt the same?'

Bella's own smile was a little strained. 'You'd have to ask him that.'

She was very convincing, Josh thought bitterly, and he was almost relieved when Aisling moved to a chair slightly behind him and drew him out of the circle.

'I just wanted to thank you for taking it all so well, Josh,' she said under cover of the general conversation. 'You could have made it very difficult for me to come on this trip with Bryn if you'd wanted to.'

'There's no point in that,' said Josh, feeling curiously detached. It was hard to believe that this was a woman he had slept with, a woman he had planned to spend the rest of his life with. 'We're still working together after all,' he pointed out, 'and I want us both to be able to concentrate on winning this contract. It's not just your job that depends on it.'

Aisling looked a little daunted by his matter-of-fact attitude. He was obviously supposed to be broken-hearted by her rejection. 'I hope you know I never meant to hurt you,' she said.

'Don't worry about it,' said Josh briskly. 'I'm glad you seem so happy.'

'I am. I hope you will be, too.'

Involuntarily, Josh glanced at Bella, deep in conversation with Sally and completely oblivious of him.

Aisling followed his gaze. 'You know, Josh, it would have been a terrible mistake if I had married you,' she said. 'Bella would always have been there between us.'

'Bella's not like that at all,' he objected furiously.

'Maybe she isn't, but she would have come between us all the same,' said Aisling. 'I wasn't at all surprised when you said that you were bringing her in my place. I always thought you had always been much more in love with her than you wanted to admit.'

Josh felt as if he had walked smack into a wall in the dark, leaving him jarred and disorientated. 'That's rubbish,' he said unevenly. 'Bella and I are just good friends. We always have been and we always will be. You've seen us together, Aisling. You know there's no question of anything else.'

Aisling smiled faintly as she got up. 'Isn't there?' she said.

Josh stared after her. In *love* with Bella? No, he couldn't be! Aisling didn't know what she was talking about. He loved Bella, of course, the same way he loved his sister.

Except that he never knew whether his sister had been in the room just by the fragrance in the air, did he? He couldn't close his eyes and conjure up his sister's image down to the last tilt of her lashes. And, fond as he was of her, he never felt better just knowing that his sister was there.

The way he did with Bella.

Oh, God, he *was* in love with her!

It was as if the world had suddenly tilted, leaving Josh

sliding and slipping towards a precipitous drop, and struggling frantically to claw his way back to safe ground where Bella was just the same as she had always been.

When had it happened? Had she changed, or had he?

'What did Aisling want?' Bella broke into his reeling thoughts and Josh stared at her stupidly.

'She just…'

Just wanted to blow his life apart. To rock the foundations of his world. To throw everything he thought he felt about his best friend into doubt.

'… she just wanted to thank me,' he said, astounded that his voice came out sounding almost normal.

'What for?'

'For understanding how she felt about Bryn. She said she was grateful.'

'As well she might be,' Bella sniffed, remembering the emerald ring Aisling was still flaunting. At least she had had the decency to wear it on her right hand.

That had been a very intimate chat the two of them had been having, though, and Josh had looked shell-shocked when Aisling had walked away. 'Did she say anything else?'

Josh hesitated. 'Only that she thought it would have been a terrible mistake if we had got married.'

'She would say that, wouldn't she? Mind you, she's not the only one that thinks so,' Bella told him. 'I've just been talking to Sally there. She says she's worked with you a couple of times and that she likes you a lot but she was never mad about Aisling when she was at C.B.C. She told me that she'd heard rumours that the two of you had got together, and she said she was glad when she met me to find out that it wasn't true.'

'What did you say?'

It was Bella's turn to hesitate. 'Well, I thought I'd better let her believe that she'd misunderstood, so I said that you were mine and always had been.'

She laughed to show that she hadn't really meant it, and then she made the mistake of looking into Josh's eyes again, and the desperate expression she saw there made her heart stop for a second. She had never seen Josh look like that before.

'Are you OK?'

'Yes…' He shook his head as if to clear it. 'It was just something Aisling said…' He stopped, unable to continue.

A tide of shame and guilt surged through Bella. What had she been thinking of, joking about their pretend relationship and making snippy comments about Aisling when it was all still so raw for Josh? She had forgotten how he might feel about seeing Aisling again. He was so cool and self-contained that it was easy to forget that he might not be nearly as fine as he claimed to be, but she of all people should have known better.

'I'm sorry, Josh,' she said, contrite.

That strange expression flickered in his eyes again. 'It's not your fault,' he said.

What had Aisling said to him? Even she wouldn't be tactless enough to ask, thought Bella, but it must have been something that had made the whole situation come home to him.

She hated the bleakness in his face, couldn't bear the thought of him hurting like that. 'It'll be all right, Josh,' she tried to reassure him, putting a hand on his knee.

Josh just looked at her oddly. 'Will it?' he said.

The hotel was wedged between a steep mountainside covered in luxuriant vegetation and a curve of dazzling white sand edging the Indian Ocean. The shallows sighing onto the shore were the palest minty green, deepening to an impossible blue further out into the bay. Bella couldn't help gasping when she saw it. After London in November, it was hard to believe that it was real.

The bus from the airport emptied them out into a cool, dim bar furnished in dark tropical wood and open on two sides to catch any breeze from the sea. There they were greeted by a representative from C.B.C. who introduced herself as Cassandra and bustled around the party, ticking them officiously off her list.

'Josh Kingston…?' she echoed when it was Josh and Bella's turn. She ran her pen down the clipboard. 'Kingston, Kingston, Kingston…ah! Here you are. You're down as plus one!' She laughed merrily and looked at Bella. 'This is your wife, is it?'

'My fiancée,' said Josh curtly. 'Bella Stevenson.'

Cassandra swooped on Bella's ring. 'How gorgeous!' she gushed, brandishing a diamond of her own under Bella's nose. 'I'm getting married myself next year. We must get together and compare notes.'

Bella couldn't think of anything she would want to do less, but she smiled politely. 'We haven't started thinking about the wedding yet,' she said. 'We've only just got engaged.'

'Oh, I'll be able to give you lots of ideas,' Cassandra promised. 'I've got a few magazines with me too. You can read them on the beach.'

What could she say? I won't be needing any bridal magazines? 'That would be lovely,' said Bella dutifully.

Delighted at the prospect of long, girly chats on the subject closest to her heart, Cassandra beamed at them both. 'You're going to love your room. It is *so* romantic!'

It *was* romantic—or it would have been under different circumstances. Like Josh not pining for Aisling, for instance, thought Bella with an inward sigh. It was all clean wood and crisp linen, and sliding doors opened onto a little veranda with steps down to the beach.

The first thing Bella saw, though, was the big double bed, with frangipani blossoms laid invitingly on the pillows.

'Very romantic,' she said to Josh as she looked at everything except the bed. She was trying to sound light-hearted and amused at the situation, but wasn't quite sure that she was carrying it off. 'Cassandra was right.'

Picking up one of the frangipani flowers, she held it to her nose and breathed in the exotic perfume. 'It's a pity they didn't throw in a free bottle of champagne while they were at it. If we're going to pretend to be engaged we might as well enjoy some of the perks!'

There was no response from Josh, and when she glanced at him under her lashes she saw that he was looking preoccupied and seemed hardly to have heard her. Clearly her attempts to lighten the atmosphere weren't working.

She should just shut up, thought Bella dully. All Cassandra's talk of weddings and romantic rooms must have been all too bitter a reminder of what things might have been like if Aisling had been with him.

She had been hoping that things would be easier once the long flight was over. Sitting so close to Josh but unable to touch him had been a nightmare. Bella hadn't been able to keep her eyes off him. She tried to concentrate on her book but it was hopeless when her gaze kept sliding sideways, skittering over his severe profile, between the creases at the edge of his eye and down the hard, exciting line of his cheek to his jaw and then to the pulse that beat in his throat.

Bella would wrench her eyes away, only to find them wandering hungrily back to his shoulder, down his sleeve to his forearm and his wrist and those strong, square hands,

and her stomach would disappear in a sickening lurch of
desire. She wanted to snuggle closer, to kiss her way along
his jaw and nuzzle his neck. To put her arms around him
and cling to the solid strength of him until he kissed her
back.

Gulping, Bella forced herself to start reading the same
page of her book all over again.

At one point she must have nodded off in spite of herself, because when she stirred and blinked, it was to find
that her head was resting against his shoulder. Josh had
obviously had no trouble resisting the urge to put his arm
around her and shift her into a more comfortable position.

Fighting the temptation to press closer to him anyway,
Bella willed herself not to move. At least this way she was
touching him. But when she lifted her eyes cautiously, she
could see that Josh's jaw was clenched, and that he was
staring blindly at the seat back in front of him, his mouth
clamped shut in a rigid line, and she straightened abruptly
to move away from him.

Whatever Aisling had said had touched him on the raw.
This was no time to be snuggling up to him, Bella told
herself. She would have to give Josh time to come to terms
with losing Aisling, and it would probably be easier for
him if she kept her distance rather than constantly reminding him that he was with the wrong woman.

Bella cast a doubtful look at the bed. She wasn't sure
how she was going to keep her distance tonight. It wasn't
that big.

She sighed. She would just have to worry about that
when the time came. There was no point in wishing that
he wanted to be with her, or imagining what it would be
like if they were lovers, if they had been able to fall laugh-

ing onto the bed as soon as the door was closed, kissing as they undressed to make love with the sound of the ocean shushing onto the beach beyond the veranda.

In the meantime, she should just leave Josh alone.

CHAPTER SEVEN

JOSH had barely glanced at the bed. He had opened the sliding doors and was standing watching the sea through the coconut palms, and something in the set of his shoulders made Bella's throat ache. She couldn't bear him being this unhappy.

Quietly she went out to join him and for a while they watched the sunlight rippling over the shallows in silence. 'It looks beautiful, doesn't it?' said Bella at last. 'Do you fancy a swim?'

'Not right now,' said Josh. 'I think I'll have a shower instead.'

'OK,' she said brightly. 'Well…I think I'll go.'

It was almost as if he was deliberately trying to avoid her. Bella told herself that it was stupid to feel hurt as she changed into her bikini and slathered on sun cream. It was so long since she had seen the sun that she would burn to a crisp if she wasn't careful.

For the first time ever she felt self-conscious about her body. Josh had seen her in a bikini loads of times, and in the past she wouldn't have given a moment's thought to sashaying past him down to the beach just as she was.

But that was then and this was now, and everything seemed different. Bella dug around in her case until she found a sarong, and wrapped it tightly around her, knotting it under her arms before she went back out onto the veranda.

'See you later then,' she said as casually as she could.

'OK.' Josh's voice was tight. He watched her disappear

past the coconut palms onto the soft, white sand, and reappear a few moments later through another gap in the trees. She had unwound her sarong and was wading into the shallows in her bikini, while the light bounced off the water and over her skin.

He looked down at his hands. They were shaking. God, how was he going to get through this week?

It was all Aisling's fault. If she had kept her mouth shut, he could have carried on as he had before, confused and unsettled by this new and intense physical awareness of Bella, but able to tell himself that he was just upset about Aisling's rejection and not thinking clearly.

He couldn't do that now. Everything was too clear. Until Aisling had pointed it out, he hadn't let himself question the depth of his feeling for Bella, but of course she was right. Of course he was in love with Bella, and probably always had been. As long as he could tell himself that he loved her as friend, everything had been fine, but now that the truth was out there he couldn't deny it any longer: he didn't just love Bella, he needed her and wanted her and his hands itched to explore her, unlock her, and make her properly his.

Only he couldn't even let himself *think* about that. Bella had been very clear that she had come to support him as a friend. He couldn't turn round and take advantage of her now, especially not when he knew how she still felt about Will.

And even if he could tell her he loved her, why would she believe him? He had to be pretty fickle to be engaged to one woman on Friday morning and in love with another on Monday, Josh reminded himself ruefully. If Aisling hadn't decided that her love for Bryn was too strong to resist, he would have married her.

Or would he? Their engagement had always had an air

of unreality about it for Josh. Aisling's suggestion that they marry had seemed to make sense at the time. Now he could see that Aisling had merely been desperate to put Bryn behind her, but at the time the way the whole thing had ballooned out of control had been alarming. Josh didn't resent her. He was just glad the truth had come out before it was too late.

And now he couldn't think about anything but Bella, about the way she smiled and the way she moved, about the soft warmth of her body and the tantalising sheen of her skin and the silky, spun-gold hair. About the allure of her eyes and that wonderfully dirty laugh and the scent that drifted in the air long after she had gone.

It had taken an heroic effort of will not to put his arm around her when she was sleeping against his shoulder in the plane, and even worse torture to have to stand out here and let her walk past him in that damned sarong that was just asking to be untied so that he could spin her free of it and pull her back into the room and down onto the cool, inviting bed.

And tonight he had to get in there beside her and pretend that she was just a friend. How was he supposed to do that?

The contract. Josh told himself to focus on that. He was here to work and that was what he would do. If he con-centrated hard enough on winning the contract then maybe he would get his thoughts back under control. He would stop thinking about lying next to Bella at night and what it would be like to reach for her, and he would start re-membering that she was just a dear friend who was only here because she felt sorry for him.

Maybe.

When Bella found him later, he was sitting in the bar with Aisling, papers spread out on the table in front of them. After realising that he was hanging around like a besotted fool waiting for Bella to come back, Josh had made himself go out, where he bumped into Aisling. Since she was on her own, too, they taken the opportunity to go through their strategy for the week and decide the key points to be made and which executives needed to be targeted particularly.

Josh was feeling better. Having a shower and getting back to work had been just what he needed. Luckily Aisling was keen to get on with things too and it had taken no time at all to re-establish a good working relationship. In fact, it was already hard to remember that they had ever had any other kind of relationship.

Josh was just congratulating himself on getting a grip when Bella walked barefoot into the bar. The sarong was tied around her waist now, and her hair hung damp and tangled from the sea down her bare back. Inevitably, she had collected a group of friends on the beach, and they were laughing as they headed to the bar without noticing Josh and Aisling in the corner.

Josh didn't recognise any of the people she was with, but he recognised the lustful expression on the men's faces when they looked at Bella all right, and he scowled. She ought to go and put some more clothes on.

'Sorry,' he said to Aisling, 'what were you saying?'

They tried to carry on working, but it was hard to concentrate when the others were obviously having such a good time. When they all had a drink, they headed over to a table in the shade looking out over the beach, and it was only then that Bella saw Josh and Aisling.

She stopped, murmured something to her new friends and then padded over in her bare feet. 'Where's Bryn?' she asked coolly.

'Sleeping,' said Aisling. 'He's used to travelling business class, so he couldn't get comfortable in those economy seats.'

'How terrible for him,' said Bella, who had never been in business class and had still found the seats incredibly uncomfortable. 'I'm surprised you didn't upgrade if things were that bad.'

'One of the purposes of this week is to build team spirit,' Aisling pointed out with equally insincere sweetness. 'Obviously Bryn could see that as one of the senior executives here it wouldn't look very supportive if he didn't travel with the rest of the group.'

Bella was unimpressed by Bryn's sacrifice. She glanced at Josh. 'It looks as if you're working, so I won't disturb you,' she said as she turned to go. 'See you later.'

Josh followed her with his eyes as she carried her glass over to join the others on long rattan sofas arranged around a low table. Two of the men shifted along to make space on the sofa between them when they saw Bella approaching.

They probably couldn't believe their luck, thought Josh sourly. One of them was short and balding, the other had a distinct paunch. Weren't these guys all supposed to have wives with them?

Beside him, Aisling sighed. 'Why don't you just tell her how you feel?' she asked in a resigned voice.

'What do you mean?'

'Look at you, you can't take your eyes off her!' said Aisling with an edge of exasperation. 'Just tell her that you love her.'

'I can't,' said Josh as if the words were wrenched out of him. 'She's in love with someone else, and even if she wasn't, I don't want to risk our friendship.'

Aisling looked at him curiously. 'Odd,' she commented, 'you've spent most of your career putting yourself into dangerous situations and taking risks when you had to. I wouldn't have said you were an emotional coward either. You were prepared to take a risk on me, weren't you?'

'It's not the same.'

'Isn't Bella worth a risk?'

Josh stared out at the pool where an energetic game of water polo was in progress. 'She's too important to me to risk anything,' he said, and knew that it was true. 'I don't want to lose her.'

'Maybe she feels the way you do,' said Aisling. 'Have you thought of that? She certainly doesn't like *me* one little bit. I think she's jealous.'

'That's just Bella being protective. She thinks you've hurt me,' he told her. 'No, she's told me how she feels about Will. She has to get over him first, and I have to help her do that, not throw our whole friendship into question just when she needs it most.'

It was time to change the subject. Josh picked up one of the papers in front of him. 'Let's run over that last point again…'

But it was impossible to concentrate with all the hilarity at Bella's table, and eventually Josh had to give in. Aisling was distracted and every time he heard Bella's laugh he lost track of what he was supposed to be saying.

'Come on,' he said, stacking the papers neatly together with a sigh. 'We might as well join the others.'

He bought Aisling a drink at the bar, and they made their way over to the table, where he glared at one of the men whose thigh was a little too close to Bella's for comfort until he shifted over and asked if Josh would like to sit next to Bella. Clearly Josh was expected to say no, he was fine where he was.

'Thanks,' said Josh, squashing himself determinedly in beside her. Then he wished that he hadn't. Her body was tantalisingly close and warm. She had a glow from the sun already and he could see where the sea salt had dried on her back.

The sarong covered her legs, which was something, Josh supposed, but her midriff and arms and shoulders were bare. Next to him in his conventional trousers and short-sleeved shirt she seemed lush and exotic and practically naked. *Not* a thought which Josh needed to have right then.

She was leaning forward, her face animated and her smile burning at the edge of his vision. Josh found his hands clenching. He wanted everyone to disappear, to leave him alone with her so that he could ease her down onto batik cushions and make love to her...

'Hi, everybody! Sorry, Josh, did I make you jump?' Cassandra patted him on the shoulder from behind, amused by the way she had broken into his thoughts. 'Are you all having a lovely time?

'I'm glad I've got a few of you together,' she went on without waiting for an answer, and waved her clipboard vaguely. 'I need to let the diving instructors know who wants to sign up for their course. That starts first thing tomorrow for those of you who are interested. I can arrange deep-sea fishing as well if anyone wants that, and later in the week we'll be organising some boat trips out to other islands.'

Pausing for breath, she looked expectantly around the group. 'So, who's for diving?'

'Not me,' said Bella firmly. 'I'm happy on the beach with a book.'

Cassandra winked. 'I'll bring you some more mags tomorrow,' she promised. 'What about the rest of you?'

'I know Bryn's keen to go deep-sea fishing,' said Aisling, 'but I'd like to learn how to dive.'

'Great!' said Cassandra enthusiastically, scribbling down Aisling's name. 'Anyone else?'

Josh hesitated, but at that moment Bella shifted to reach for her drink and her bare arm pressed against his for a moment, which made him make up his mind abruptly. The further away he was from Bella at the moment the better.

'I'll go diving, too,' he told Cassandra.

Bella swung round to stare at him. 'But you know how to dive!' she objected. 'You don't have to go on a course.'

'I haven't done it for a while,' he said. 'There's no harm in a refresher course.'

'OK, so I've got Josh and Aisling,' said Cassandra. 'Any more takers?'

Most of the others opted to relax on the beach like Bella rather than sign up for any strenuous activity.

'I get enough of that at home looking after the kids,' sighed one weary mother.

'So that's just Josh and Aisling for diving,' Cassandra concluded, having been round them all. 'We'll see if we can find some others as chaperones so you and Bryn don't need to worry, Bella!' she added with an extremely irritating laugh.

'I'm not worried,' lied Bella, who in fact was furious with Josh. Why didn't he make things easier on himself by keeping out of temptation's way? If he wanted to make a fool of himself by following Aisling around with his tongue hanging out when anyone could see she was mad about Bryn, that was his problem, but he might at least think about how he was making *her* look.

'I must say I admire you for being independent,' said one of her new friends from the beach. 'When I was engaged I spent my whole time trailing after my husband and doing the things he liked rather than what I liked, just because I was terrified of what he might get up to if I wasn't there to keep an eye on him!'

'Oh, I never think about that.' Bella put a possessive hand on Josh's knee, which seemed like a suitably adoring thing to do until she felt his instinctive flinch. Mortified, she snatched her hand back. Why not stand up and shout that he didn't like her touching her?

Tough, she thought. She was trying to act a role here, even if he didn't have a clue about how a fiancé behaved. Defiantly, she put her hand back again. 'I know Josh would never be unfaithful,' she told the others. 'Would you, sweetie?'

Josh would hate being called 'sweetie'. It served him right, thought Bella. If he would just relax and behave naturally with her instead of recoiling at her slightest touch she might not have to resort to cute names.

'No,' he said in a voice that sounded oddly hoarse. He cleared his throat and started again. 'Never.'

Well, that was a *bit* better, Bella allowed grudgingly.

Cassandra had put away her clipboard and had squeezed onto the sofa opposite. 'Did you get a chance to look at that magazine I gave you on the beach, Bella?' she asked, leaning across.

'I did. It was very interesting.' Bella was rather embarrassed by the fact that she had been riveted by a copy of *Bride* that Cassandra had insisted on thrusting into her hands. She had always felt that it was vaguely unlucky to look at a magazine like that unless you were actually planning a wedding, but now that she had the perfect excuse to read it, it seemed a pity not to...

'It had some great ideas, I thought,' she told Cassandra, and glanced speculatively at Josh under her lashes. Her hand was still on his thigh, and it was obviously making him tense.

'I've been wondering whether we should go for a themed wedding,' she said. 'You know, the Arabian Nights or something. We could decorate the marquee as a desert tent with rugs and brass lamps, and I could have lots of veils. Josh could be dressed as a sheikh. What do you think, Josh?'

'Over my dead body,' he said.

Bella pretended to pout. 'Oh, I thought it would be fun to bring out your unconventional side,' she said. 'And it would be appropriate, too. You have spent a lot of time in deserts.'

'I've also spent lot of time in England,' Josh pointed out, and Bella was secretly relieved to hear the crispness return to his voice. 'I'm quite happy staying in touch with my conventional side, thank you very much. A morning suit is as wacky as I'm prepared to go.'

The very idea of Josh in a morning suit gave Bella a pang and she forced her mind away from imagining him in the local church where her parents lived, waiting for her to arrive—and there was no use pretending she hadn't picked out exactly the dress she wanted from Cassandra's magazine—and tuned back into the conversation.

Cassandra was explaining how she was planning a traditional wedding, 'But there's going to be an overall sea theme. The bridesmaids and pageboys are going to be in little sailor suits, there'll be shells on the table and even the place cards are going to be decorated with starfish.'

'Wow,' said Bella. Clearly behind Cassandra's fluffy exterior lurked the organisational abilities of a brigadier. 'When is the wedding?'

'Not till next year. What about you?'

Never, the way things were going. Still, she had better stay in her role, thought Bella, snuggling perversely into

Josh and risking a kiss on his jaw. 'The sooner the better as far as we're concerned. That's right, isn't it, Josh?'

'Yes,' he said abruptly, and then ruined what little credibility he had as a fiancé by literally shaking her off as he stood up. 'It's getting late,' he said. 'We should go and get ready for the reception this evening.'

Aisling got to her feet as well. 'Yes, I'd better go too and wake Bryn.'

Right. Why not announce to the world that they wanted an excuse to snatch a few more minutes alone?

Already humiliated by Josh's brusque rejection, Bella's eyes flashed dangerously. He had pointedly not held out his hand to help her up and include her in his unilateral decision to go and get ready, but he needn't think that she was going to sit here tamely while he went mooning after Aisling. They had already had quite enough of a tête-à-tête ''working'', as they called it, in the bar.

Bella's lips tightened and she drained her glass. She was here as Josh's fiancée, and that's how he should treat her. 'I'll come with you,' she said. 'I want a shower before dinner.'

She took a childish delight in making him take her hand as they left the bar with Aisling, but the moment they were out of sight of the others, he dropped it abruptly. Bella hugged her arms miserably around her to give her hands something to do.

They left Aisling at the door to her room, then walked across the grounds in tense silence. The sun was dropping down to the horizon, staining the sky pink and orange and there was a hushed, expectant feel to the air. Even the ocean seemed to have gone quiet as it waited for the night to fall.

It was such a waste to be miserable in such a romantic place, thought Bella. Even if she and Josh went back to being friends, it would be better than this. They needed to relax and to talk, she decided.

'Shall we walk along the beach?' she suggested, thinking that even Josh couldn't resist the appeal of a tropical beach at sunset.

Apparently he could. 'I thought you wanted a shower?' he said.

'I do, but there's no hurry.'

'You should have stayed in the bar with the others,' he said, an edge to his voice. 'You seemed to be having a good time.'

Bella was rapidly losing patience. 'I would have done,' she said tartly, 'but I haven't forgotten that I'm supposed to be here as your fiancée, and no self-respecting fiancée would be happy about letting her man stroll off into the sunset with another woman.'

Josh made an exasperated noise. 'We weren't strolling anywhere. Aisling was on her way back to her room. You know that.'

'I might do, but it doesn't look that way to everyone else. People are already commenting on how much time the two of you spend together, and we've only been here a few hours!'

They had reached their room and Josh fished the key out of his shirt pocket. 'You just need to tell them that Aisling and I work together,' he said impatiently as he unlocked the door.

'It would take more than that to stop them speculating,' said Bella, stalking into the room. 'I think they're beginning to wonder who exactly it is that you're engaged to. You certainly don't seem to want to spend any time with me!'

'For God's sake, Bella, you're the one who said we've only been here a few hours!'

'Look,' she said, unfastening her sarong, too cross by this stage to feel self-conscious about her body in front of him. 'I'm just saying that you don't seem to be a very convincing fiancé.' In spite of herself, Bella was unable to keep the hurt from her voice. 'You flinch if I touch you, jump at the chance to spend your days with another woman, and generally don't want anything to do with me. There's not much point in my being here if you're going to carry on like that!'

They glared at each other until Josh suddenly blew out a breath and ran a hand through his short hair in a gesture of weariness. 'I'm sorry, Bella,' he sighed. 'You're right. I'm no good at pretending, that's all.'

Bella's exasperation evaporated at the defeated expression on his face. Josh's inability to keep away from Aisling might hurt her, but she knew just how he felt, didn't she?

'No, it's my fault,' she said gently. 'I know it's a difficult situation for you, Josh. It's easy to say that you should get on with your life, and that there's no point torturing yourself by being with the person you love when you know they don't love you and that you can't have them, but if you really love someone, you can't just give up like that.'

She hesitated, wanting to put her arms round him, but not trusting herself if she did. 'I do understand, you know.'

'It sounds as if you do,' he said heavily.

'I hope this week isn't going to be too hard for you,' said Bella. She had thrown her sarong over a chair and dressed only in her bikini was looking through her case for a brush.

Josh looked at her, warm and vivid and practically naked in the room with the double bed between them.

'I think it will be,' he said. 'I think it'll be a lot harder than I ever expected.'

Bella sat on the edge of the bed and threw her hair down over her face to brush it vigorously. In spite of all the lotions and potions she had spent a fortune on and which promised that her hair would be a silken, shining gold curtain at all times it had dried into a salty tangle.

'You know, I don't think you should give up,' she said, proud of how steady her voice sounded. 'I mean, it's obvious that Aisling still likes you a lot. She might be wrapped up in Bryn now, but he's such a prat, isn't he? I only talked to him for a few minutes, but that was enough to find him deeply irritating. And did you see how he was swanking around at Heathrow? I wouldn't be surprised if a week in his company is enough for Aisling to come to her senses and send him back to his wife—who is probably extremely glad to be rid of him!'

Confident that she had her face back under control, Bella straightened and tossed her hair back over her shoulders. 'When that happens, she's bound to turn back to you,' she told Josh, who was standing looking out at the rapidly gathering darkness, his hands in his pockets and his shoulders slightly hunched.

'So I just have to be patient?' he said.

'If that's what you want.'

He turned abruptly. 'What about you, Bella? I haven't been great company for you so far. I'm sorry.'

'Don't worry, I understand, and it's fine.' She smiled brightly as she got up and began unpacking her case. 'I'm having a great time. Most of the people seem really nice, I'm staying in this fabulous hotel for free, and I've got a whole week to lie in the sun and read. What more could I want?'

'Will?' suggested Josh.

Bella froze for a second, then busied herself hanging clothes in the wardrobe. It made a good reason to turn her

face away so that Josh couldn't read her expression too
clearly.

'We can't always have everything we want,' she said.
'Sometimes we just have to make the most of what we've
got.'

Josh thought about what she had said as he lay sleepless
beside her that night. Moonlight slipped into the room
through a crack in the curtains and laid a stripe across
Bella, who lay on her front, her face turned towards the
window and her hair spilling over the pillow. The light
was a bright band, highlighting the curve of her shoulder,
and grazing the edge of her mouth. It lit the soft line of
her cheek and turned her hair silver before striping on
across the pillow and up the wall.

Was this the only way he could look at her properly
now? Josh wondered in despair. When she was asleep?

She had looked wonderful earlier at the reception laid
on by C.B.C. to welcome everyone, but Josh hadn't been
able to gaze at her the way he had wanted to do. There
were too many other people around, too many others vying
for her attention, too many of them standing between him
and Bella.

She had been wearing some kind of sleeveless red dress
and yet another pair of absurdly fragile shoes. Josh didn't
know very much about women's clothes, but he could see
that the outfit made Bella the sparkling centre of the room.
Amongst the muted colours everyone else seemed to be
wearing, she stood out like a bright flame.

Torn between pride and jealousy, Josh watched her flirting and charming her way around the room. Apparently it
was all right for *her* to ignore *him*, he had thought sourly,
remembering her earlier complaints.

But it was hard not to admire her. She had been with
these people less than twenty-four hours, and already she

seemed to know everybody, and whether by design or not, had contrived to make firm friends with a number of the key people who would make the final decision about whether to award Josh the global contract or not. They kept coming up to Josh and telling him how nice Bella was, how pretty she was, what fun.

As if he didn't know.

He should have been pleased. He should have been grateful. He should have encouraged Bella. Josh knew all that. But all he really wanted to do was to push his way through the men thronging around her, grab her by the wrist and drag her back to the room. Instead he had to smile and agree that, yes, Bella was a very special person.

The dinner after the reception was nearly as bad, and then there was sitting around in the bar to be got through. Josh found himself longing for the moment when he would have Bella to himself, but when they finally left to go back to their room, it was even worse.

Once they would have laughed and compared notes about who they had met, and Bella would have conducted an extensive critique of what the other women had been wearing, the intricacies of which Josh had never really appreciated but which had always amused him. But now any attempt at conversation shrivelled in the air and the only sound to break the silence between them as they walked back to their room was the rasp of insects in the tropical darkness.

They were both determinedly matter-of-fact about going to bed. Josh had looked out some old pyjama bottoms and Bella was wearing a nightdress she had obviously chosen for its lack of seductive frills but whose uncharacteristic plainness only emphasised the glow of her skin and hinted at the lushness of her body beneath.

Josh waited on the veranda, listening to the insects and

the murmur of sea, and trying not to think about peeling
that nightdress off Bella, while she spent what seemed like
hours in the bathroom. His turn took a couple of minutes
and, by the time he came out, she was in bed, the sheet
pulled up to her chin.

'Are you cold?' he asked stiltedly. 'I can turn the air-
conditioning down if you like.'

'No, I'm fine.'

Tightening his jaw, Josh threw back the sheets on his
side and got in. He could lie without touching Bella at all,
but he was desperately aware of how close she was.

'Are you ready for me to switch off the light?' he asked
in a voice that didn't sound like his at all.

'Yes, thanks.'

One click, and the room was plunged into darkness, with
just the sound of the air-conditioning rattling into the silence.

Josh cleared his throat. 'Well, this is odd,' he said.

'I know.' Bella sounded grateful to him for breaking the
silence. 'It's lucky we're such good friends, isn't it?
Imagine what it was like for Phoebe and Gib. They ended
up sharing a bed with someone they didn't really know at
all. It must have been really awkward.'

Josh wondered how it could possibly have felt more
awkward than it felt now, lying next to Bella and knowing
that whatever he did he mustn't reach for her.

'Lucky for us,' he agreed dryly.

CHAPTER EIGHT

JOSH hoped that things would get easier as the week went by, but they didn't really. The days weren't too bad. He spent most of his time diving, and in the evenings he was careful not to be alone with Bella if he could avoid it. She was always the centre of a big group anyway, so that wasn't a problem.

That meant that there were only the nights to get through. Josh told himself to treat them as an endurance test, like sitting out a blizzard halfway up a mountain, or carrying a heavy pack through the jungle when there were leeches insinuating themselves into your socks and you hadn't slept for three nights. If he could survive those, he could survive this.

Of course he could.

Aisling provided the most effective cover for his feelings for Bella, and Josh stuck as close to her as he could. It wasn't difficult. Bryn had turned out to be obsessive about deep-sea angling, and while Josh and Aisling were diving, he was out on a boat, strapped into a chair, and wrestling with, according to him at least, monster fish. In the evenings, he would relive his exploits in second by second accounts of his machismo to anyone who would listen.

Josh noticed that Aisling looked a little tight-lipped at times, and often manoeuvred to a join the table where he and Bella were sitting rather than sit alone with Bryn, and he began to wonder if Bella's theory was right and that Aisling's passionate romance was wearing thin already.

'I told you so.' Bella was almost snappy when he mentioned it to her. 'It must make you feel better.'

Better? Josh was puzzled for moment before remembering that he was supposed to be still in love with Aisling.

'Oh…yes, yes, it does,' he lied.

'Obviously all those hours you and Aisling spend diving are paying off,' said Bella with a brittle smile. 'I'm very happy for you.'

'You don't sound very happy.'

'No, well, it's hard to feel very happy about being dumped on the beach every day while you and Aisling go off together,' she snapped.

Josh looked at her in surprise. 'You said didn't want to go diving,' he reminded her. 'You said were having a good time.'

'It's not much fun being an object of pity for everyone else on the beach!'

He frowned. 'What do you mean?'

'You know what I mean, Josh!' said Bella angrily. 'I know you want to be with Aisling, and that's fine, but you might give some thought to what it's like for me stuck here all day. Everyone thinks we're about to split up.'

'What?'

'Of course they do! They see you with Aisling, never with me. We never do anything together.'

Bella was appalled at how close she was to tears. She had been trying so hard not to mind when Josh went off with Aisling every day. Nor had Aisling's growing impatience with Bryn been lost on her.

Any day now, Aisling was going to realise what she had lost when she left Josh for Bryn. With Josh so clearly still available and keen to get back together, she wouldn't hesitate to say something to him, and then what was going to happen to *her*? Bella wondered. She would have to try and be happy for Josh but she wasn't sure that she would be able to bear it.

She was in a crowd all day, and at night she lay stiffly next to Josh, yearning to be able to touch him. She was never alone and she had never felt lonelier. Josh was scrupulously polite but it was clear how he felt. Once she had rolled over and brushed against him by mistake, and he had flinched.

'Sorry,' she had muttered, horribly embarrassed, and huddled back to her own side of the bed.

What was it Josh had said about the week turning out to be even harder than he had expected? Now Bella knew exactly what he meant. She didn't know whether she longed for the week to be over, or dreaded it as the last chance she might have to be this close to Josh.

He was looking apologetic now. 'The diving course finishes tomorrow,' he said. 'Maybe we could do something together on Friday?'

Some of the others had hired jeeps and found secluded beaches or great little fish restaurants. 'OK,' said Bella, trying desperately not to sound too eager, but unable to stop her heart quickening in anticipation of some time alone with him. At least she could make the most of it before Aisling realised just what a mistake she had made in letting him go.

'Aisling says there's a boat trip out to some of the uninhabited outer islands then,' Josh said. 'There'll be a chance to go snorkelling, too. We could go on that together if you like.'

Sick disappointment twisted in Bella's stomach. It sounded as if he couldn't bear the thought of a day without Aisling. She was furious with herself for that brief moment of excitement, but if she objected, she would sound like a spoilt, sulky child.

'Sure,' she said dully.

In spite of her disappointment, her spirits rose on Friday morning. Josh had breakfast with her and there was no sign of Aisling. Maybe she had changed her mind, thought Bella hopefully. Meanwhile, the day stretched ahead of them, a whole day with Josh. They might not be alone, but at least he would be there. The way Bella felt at that moment, it would be enough.

And it was a beautiful day. The sky was a deep, cloudless blue, the sea still and translucent, and the early morning sun behind the palm trees threw ragged shadows on the white sand. It was a picture of paradise, thought Bella. Impossible to feel depressed in a place like this on a day like this.

To hell with Aisling, she decided defiantly. I'm going to enjoy today whether she's there or not.

Unfortunately, Aisling *was* there. When the rest of them arrived, she was waiting down by the jetty with Bryn, who had obviously been persuaded to take a day off from killing fish and looked as if he was regretting it already.

There were eleven of them altogether, including Cassandra. Having spent the week organising trips for everyone else, she felt she was entitled to go on one herself, she explained.

'Now, is everyone here?'

She began counting heads, while Josh frowned at the boat tied up by the jetty. 'Are we going in that?' he interrupted her.

'What's wrong with it?'

'It's very open and very low—and it's going to get even lower when we all get in it,' he pointed out.

Bryn strolled over to join in the discussion. 'What's the problem?'

'I'm just a bit concerned about the lack of protection,'

said Josh, not looking as if he welcomed Bryn's input at all.

'Good God, man, there's a perfectly adequate sun-shade!'

'I wasn't thinking of the sun,' Josh said evenly. 'I'm thinking about what would happen if we ran into rough seas.'

'What rough seas?' Bryn was openly dismissive. 'The sea's like a millpond.'

Josh's slate-coloured eyes narrowed as he looked at the horizon where you could just make out a faint smudge. 'I've got a bad feeling about the weather,' he admitted.

Bryn followed his glance. 'Just a heat haze,' he pronounced. 'Come on, let's go.'

'Just a minute,' said Josh quietly, but something in his tone stopped Bryn in his tracks. 'Who's in charge of this boat?' he asked Cassandra, who was beginning to look flustered.

'It's Ron's boat. He's terribly reliable and he's done lots of trips for us before, but he can't come himself today so he's sent Elvis instead,' she said, and pointed at the boy sitting patiently at the tiller. 'He's only thirteen, but he's been helping his father on this boat since he could walk.'

'I'm sure Elvis knows what he's doing,' said Josh dryly. 'I'd just feel better if there was any sign of a life-jacket on board.'

'Oh, stop being such an old woman!' said Bryn. 'We're not going to need life-jackets on a day like today.'

'Yes, do stop fussing, Josh,' said Aisling. 'If we hang around looking for life-jackets it'll be too late to go at all.'

There was an immediate uproar from the others, and Josh found himself overruled as they piled into the boat, which promptly sank perilously low in the water. Josh didn't like it at all, but Bella, who had been chatting and hadn't heard any of the discussion, was already in. Short of dragging her out bodily, there wasn't much he could do about it, and he certainly wasn't letting her go off in a boat like this without him.

Reluctantly, Josh untied the rope for Elvis and got in as well with a last glance at the horizon. Maybe he was wrong about the weather.

For most of the day, it seemed that he was. The tarpaulin rigged over the boat gave some shade, but it was still very hot and the sea was oily and still as they puttered out to the furthermost islands. The mood was cheerful, as if everyone realised that they would be going home to winter in a couple of days and were determined to make the most of it. Only Josh kept a watchful eye on the horizon, but the smudge didn't move.

They anchored at last on a tiny exposed atoll where the coral wall fell away into deep, clear, turquoise water. Leaning over the edge of the boat, they oohed and aahed at the iridescent fish that darted in and out of the coral.

'See?' said Bryn with a sneer. 'If we'd listened to Josh, we'd still be looking for life-jackets and we wouldn't have seen this.'

Bella stood up abruptly. 'Where are the masks and flippers?' she asked, changing the subject before anyone else could jump on the jeering bandwagon Bryn was clearly intent on setting rolling. 'I don't know about the rest of you, but I want to go snorkelling before lunch.'

Josh wished that he could shake the uncanny sense of impending disaster. He was torn between watching that ominous smudge on the horizon and following Bella into the limpid water. Surely she'd be safe here? But tides could be treacherous, and sharks weren't unknown…

Suddenly afraid to let her out of his sight, Josh put on a mask and snorkel and tipped neatly into the water after the others. She had only been snorkelling once before and he caught up with her easily and shadowed her unobtrusively as she drifted happily along the reef, unaware of his presence until he touched her arm and pointed.

Bella looked to see a huge turtle swimming gracefully past, so unlike lumbering progress on land. Rapt, she watched it go then lifted her head out of the water to remove her snorkel as Josh surfaced beside her.

'Wasn't it *beautiful*? Oh, that's one of the best things I've ever seen!' She was so thrilled that Josh's unease began to recede. Bella was happy, he told himself. Everything was fine.

Not wanting to crowd her, he made his way back to the boat after a while, and sat and talked to Elvis until the others started to trickle back. Bella was one of the last. Josh saw her head pop up out of the water by the ladder and, in spite of his decision not to worry, he was conscious of a sharp sense of relief.

Throwing her flippers ahead of her into the boat, she climbed up the ladder and pulled off her mask. It left a red mark on her face and her hair was all wet and tangled, but she looked gorgeous, thought Josh. She was lit up with excitement, and bubbling with enthusiasm.

'Wasn't it fabulous? I can't believe the colours! What are those blue and yellow stripy fish called? And did you *see* the turtle?'

They were all happy and laughing, comparing notes on what they had seen and talking about lunch which the hotel had provided.

'I'm starving,' said Bella. 'Let's eat now and then we can have another snorkel later.'

She clambered over the muddle of snorkels and flippers towards Josh to retrieve her shorts and top but, just as she got there, someone else climbed onto the boat, making it rock suddenly. Losing her balance, she fell against him.

Josh caught her instinctively, and for a breathless moment he held her against him. She was still dripping, and she was warm and wet against his bare chest where their skin touched. Unable to stop his arm from tightening around her, Josh found himself looking straight into the blue eyes, and his heart missed a beat.

'OK?' he asked, dry-mouthed and shaken by how much he wanted her.

Bella nodded dumbly and jerked herself out of his arm before she did anything silly like running her hands up over his shoulders or down the broad, muscled back. She was shocked by the impact of their bare flesh, by the jolt of electric excitement that came from the briefest and most impersonal of touches.

The feel of his skin against hers was all that it took for her to forget all the careful resolutions she had made, all that deciding to make the most of what she had got, all those noble, self-sacrificing thoughts telling herself that she only wanted Josh to be happy.

Who was she trying to kid? She wanted a lot more than that. She wanted to cover him with kisses and taste the salt on his skin. She wanted to feel his hands hard against her body. She wanted him to pull her down into the mess of rubber and shoes in the bottom of the boat and make love to her there and then, and to hell with everyone else.

That would rock the boat, in more ways than one.

Swallowing hard, Bella concentrated fiercely on pulling on her clothes.

Meanwhile, Josh was trying not to think about how quickly she had pulled away from him. Had she noticed the instinctive tightening of his arm, or read the naked desire in his eyes? Was that why she had recoiled like that?

To take his mind off her, Josh turned to look at the horizon again, and stiffened. The smudge had resolved itself into an ugly black line advancing across the blue sky.

He got to his feet. 'I think we should go,' he announced.

Immediately there was a chorus of protests about lunch and wanting to stay where they were and other chances to see the turtle.

Josh cut across them. 'Look!' he said, and pointed to the blackness on the horizon.

'Oh, but it's miles away!

'It's lovely here.'

'We need to go,' said Josh. 'Now.' The authority in his voice shut them up at last. 'Who's not here?' he asked.

'Bryn,' said Aisling. 'He said he wanted to look around the other side.'

'We'd better go and find him. Did you see which way he went?'

Elvis started the motor while Josh pulled up the anchor, and they made their way slowly around the atoll looking out for Bryn's snorkel. Everyone had picked up on Josh's sense of urgency by this stage and uneasy glances were cast at the advancing black line.

'There he is!' They had wasted precious minutes before Bella spotted the snorkel poking out of the water ahead.

Elvis brought the boat up alongside Bryn, who registered their presence enough to wave but blithely carried on snorkelling.

Josh sighed. 'I'll go and get him.'

Flipping neatly over the side, he swam to intercept Bryn. They were too far away for Bella to hear what they were saying, but it was obvious that Josh was having difficulty convincing him to get back in the boat, in spite of being able to point at the menacing black sky in the distance.

Aisling was watching them anxiously. 'Can't you do anything?' said Bella. 'He'll listen to you, won't he?'

'Not if he thinks I am trying to get him to do what Josh wants him to do.' Aisling glanced at Bella. 'Bryn's jealous of Josh because…well, you know…'

Yes, Bella knew, but this didn't seem the time for petty jealousies.

Fortunately, someone shouted just then that the two men were on their way back to the boat. It was never clear exactly what Josh had said to Bryn, but judging by the expression on Bryn's face as he climbed grudgingly into the boat it was nothing very pleasant.

'I don't know what all the fuss is about,' he grumbled to Aisling. 'Those clouds are nowhere near, and anyway, I'm not afraid of a bit of tropical rain!' He jerked his head to where Josh was consulting with Elvis. 'The Kommandant over there seems to be insisting that we head back, but I don't see what's wrong with staying here.'

'There's no shelter here,' said Bella clearly.

Bryn tapped his hand against the tarpaulin. 'This'll keep off the worst of the rain. We might get a bit wet, but it'll soon pass over. These tropical downpours always do.'

'This is going to be more than a passing shower,' said Josh, overhearing him. 'It's too exposed out here. We need to get back to one of those islands we passed on the way out and try and find some shelter if we can. At least we could get off the boat. It's not designed for rough weather.'

'Well, I say we should sit out here,' said Bryn loudly, looking around the boat. 'Who agrees with me?'

Josh stepped up until he was nose to nose with him. 'We're not putting this to the vote,' he said very quietly, but in a voice that sent a little frisson down Bella's spine. She had never heard Josh talk like that before and she was very glad that his anger wasn't directed at her.

'There's a storm coming,' he went on in the same cold, clear tone. 'This boat is unsafe and as Bella pointed out, there's no shelter out here. I am not prepared to risk Bella's life, or anyone else's come to that, on the chance that this will just be a "downpour". We're not voting on anything. We are going back to that last island as fast as we can so I suggest that you just *sit* down and *shut* up.'

Bryn sat.

Josh went to sit beside Elvis, who was looking very young and very nervous by now. 'OK, Elvis,' he said, clapping him on the shoulder. 'Full steam ahead!'

'Where does he get off ordering everyone around?' Bryn muttered. 'He'll have us all goose-stepping next! If I'd known I was signing up for the army, I'd never have come on this holiday.'

'Pity you didn't,' muttered Cassandra, who was sitting next to Bella.

Bella glanced at the nervous faces around her. 'Josh knows what he's doing,' she said, more for their benefit than for Bryn's.

'Yes, shut up, Bryn,' said Aisling, looking strained.

It was very hot still. The sun beat down, bouncing and glittering on the water, and they were all glad of the awning over the boat which at least gave some shade. The sea was flat calm and so clear that you could see shoals of fish beneath the boat, flashing silver as they turned suddenly and caught the light.

There was something eerie about the idyllic scene, thought Bella. Ahead, all was calm and perfect, but if you glanced behind, as they were all doing with increasing nervousness, the blackness was creeping menacingly closer, gobbling up the blue sky, as it advanced inexorably towards them.

The boat was pegging bravely onwards. Josh looked

over his shoulder. 'Is this the fastest she can do?' he asked Elvis casually.

'Yes, sir. This is top speed already.'

'Well, don't worry, we'll just keep going as we are. It's not much further now.'

Everyone began to look more hopeful, although Bella suspected that it was more because Josh sounded positive than from any evidence that the situation was improving. She had been scanning the horizon desperately for land, and she hadn't seen any sign of an island anywhere near by. It was as if they were all, with the exception of Bryn, instinctively looking to Josh for reassurance.

'It does seem to be getting closer,' said Cassandra in a quavering voice. 'Is it going to overtake us?'

'We might get a bit wet,' Josh told her cheerfully, 'but once we get to that island we can sit it out.' He nodded at the iceboxes which contained their lunch. 'We've got food and drink, so we won't starve. We'll be fine.'

There was something incredibly reassuring about him, thought Bella. He wasn't the best-looking man on the boat, he certainly wasn't the best dresser, and he didn't have smart cars or the latest technology to flash around. But he was the one person you wanted with you in a situation like this. He was so calm, so solid, so safe. It was impossible to believe that he would let anything bad happen.

'You're doing a great job, Elvis,' he was encouraging the boy, who smiled nervously and tried to stop biting his lip and darting glances over his shoulder.

'Oh, yes, great!' said Bryn sarcastically. 'Personally, I'd save my compliments for someone who bothered to listen to the weather forecast! I'm going to have something to say to the hotel when we get back,' he huffed. 'The whole situation is outrageous. I shall demand my money back,

and suggest that they use more professional people in future for any boat trips they organise.'

Elvis was looking stricken. As if he didn't have enough
problems right now with a boatload of westerners and the
mother of all storms rushing up behind him, he could obviously see his family's livelihood disappearing as well.

Bella glared at Bryn. 'If we get back, it'll be thanks to
Elvis, not you,' she said clearly. Under cover of a smatter
of hear-hears, she leant across to Bryn, who was sitting
almost exactly opposite her. 'Now shut up about it,' she
said through her teeth. 'He's just a boy, and he's scared.'

'He's not the only one!' said Cassandra.

They were all sitting tensely, leaning forward slightly as
if to will the boat faster through the water. It was hard to
believe that only a few minutes ago they had been talking
and laughing and thinking about lunch. Now they waited
in increasingly ominous silence for the storm to catch
them.

When someone spotted an island in the distance, their
spirits rose dramatically, but just as they were congratulating themselves on the narrowness of their escape, a tiny
puff of wind lifted the oppressive heat.

Josh leapt for awning, as the puff was followed by another, and then another. 'Let's get this down!'

'But it's going to pour,' Bryn objected as the blackness
loomed. 'We won't have any shelter.'

'If the wind catches this, it'll tip us over, and keeping
dry will be the last of our problems,' said Josh.

Three of the other men had got up to help him untie the
awning while Bryn sulked, but already those first delicate
puffs of breeze had grown into a wind that was making
the task more difficult. The canvas was flapping horribly,
while the boat tilted in the choppy water and the men
staggered on their feet as they wrestled with the knots.

There were a few murmurs of distress, and Cassandra was not the only one looking suddenly white-faced.

Bella couldn't believe how suddenly the conditions had changed. One minute they had been puttering along in the flat calm and the next they were in the middle of a screaming gale. And the wind was just a foretaste of what was to come. Another second and the sun had been swallowed up by the boiling black clouds, and the rain hit them with the force of a ten-ton truck.

'Bella!' Josh had to bellow over the screaming wind and crashing rain. He had taken over the tiller from Elvis, who was frantically throwing water overboard with a ludicrously small plastic baler. 'Get everyone baling!'

Blinking through the water that streamed down her face, Bella gave Josh the thumbs up sign to show that she had understood.

How she was going to go about it was another matter. She looked around desperately before grabbing a mask from the muddle of snorkels and flippers and abandoned shoes which were already floating in the rainwater accumulating in the bottom of the boat and began baling. Not very effective, it had to be said, but it was better than nothing.

'I feel sick,' moaned Cassandra.

'Here.' Bella shoved the mask at her and groped around for another one. 'Help get rid of some of this water. You'll feel better if you've got something to do.'

Although what would *she* know? Bella asked herself wryly. Still, she had obviously convinced Cassandra who began scooping up water obediently with her mask.

Aisling had seen what they were doing and was handing out masks on the other side. Even Bryn took one. Bella wasn't sure that was a good sign. Things must look really bad for him to come out of his sulk and follow Josh's advice.

Buffeted by waves on all sides and submerging under the deluge of water, the little boat seemed to be standing still in the water. It seemed a lifetime since they had stood on the sunny jetty that morning and pooh-poohed Josh's caution about life-jackets, a lifetime of bending and scooping and chucking the water from the bottom of the boat that filled up as quickly as they could try and empty it. The rain was relentless, hammering down on them while the wind shrieked and the sea surged, slopping waves over the side and tearing at her hair.

Bella's shoulders ached with baling, but she managed to get into a rhythm eventually which made it easier. What am I doing here? she wondered. I'm a city girl. I should be at my computer or in some bar, not stuck on a sinking boat in the middle of the Indian Ocean. I do text messages and buying shoes, not survival.

Someone near her was crying, but Bella couldn't see who it was and anyway, if she had to do survival, she was going to survive, and that meant keeping on baling rather than stopping to offer comfort. She felt oddly detached. The whole thing had happened so suddenly and was so overwhelming that it seemed vaguely surreal, but beneath her surface calm she was absolutely terrified.

Whenever fear threatened to become too much, she would fix her mind on Josh. She could hardly make him out through the lashing rain, but even an indistinct glimpse of his solid figure, holding onto the tiller with one hand and baling like everyone else with the other, was enough to reassure her. Josh was there and in control, and he wouldn't let anything happen to her.

It was like being trapped in a nightmare. Bella baled and baled and baled, and forgot what it was like to feel warm and dry and safe. She was in such a zombiefied state that a shout from Elvis barely penetrated her consciousness and it wasn't until Cassandra prodded her that she looked up to see the island.

After longing for the sight of land, it loomed terrifyingly close through the driving rain, The little boat was already perilously close to the rocks that fringed the island, but still they all cheered at the sight and redoubled their efforts to stop it sinking before they could reach the shore.

After some consultation with Elvis, Josh put on his shoes and made his way cautiously to the front of the boat.

'What are you doing?' Bella shouted over the sound of the wind and rain as he passed her.

'We can't risk running the boat onto the rocks or we might never get off again,' he shouted back. 'Elvis is going to get as close as he dares, and by then it should be shallow enough for me to get in and anchor it. I can pull the boat the rest of the way.'

'You're going to jump into the sea?' Bella was horrified. 'Josh, you can't! It's too dangerous.'

His hand rested briefly on her cheek. 'Don't worry, it'll be fine.'

Bella could hardly bear to watch as he disappeared overboard. The water was wild and the wind furious, tossing the boat around spitefully. How could he even stand, let alone manoeuvre them into the shore?

It was hard to see what was going on, but those at the front of the boat passed the message back down the line that Josh's feet had touched the bottom and that he was slowly but surely, dragging them through the rocks into the shore. The waves slapped him in the face and made him stagger, but when he was knee-deep he signalled to Elvis to cut the engine and drop the anchor.

They would all have to wade the rest of the way but

they were so wet by that stage and so relieved to have reached land that no one objected, not even Bryn. Forming a chain, they passed the iceboxes, awning and various bags over their heads and then huddled together on the tiny beach.

If anything the storm seemed worse here, as if maddened by their attempt to escape its clutches. The palm trees bent almost to the ground before the force of the wind, which whipped their leaves savagely and tossed debris into the air, while the rain slashed down in a deafening torrent.

'Welcome to paradise!' Bella shouted above the tumult, and they all laughed rather hysterically.

Under the conditions, it was difficult to tell much about the island, but eventually it was decided to explore inland to see if they could rig up a rudimentary shelter with the awning.

Josh stayed behind with Elvis to see if they could make the boat more secure, but he watched Bella struggle up the beach with Cassandra, carrying an icebox between them. She was smiling encouragingly and apparently even managing to make jokes, judging by the way her companions laughed as if despite themselves.

It didn't take long to explore the island, which was rocky and covered in sparse vegetation. On the lee side Josh found another beach which was relatively sheltered, and they managed to tie the awning between some trees, where a rocky wall behind gave them the illusion of protection from the rain, although the benefit was largely psychological. By the time they had carried everything over there, they were all exhausted, and they collapsed together under the canvas with groans of relief.

CHAPTER NINE

ONLY Josh resisted the temptation to slump with the others. 'I think it would be a good idea to bring the boat round here,' he said, eyeing the beach critically. 'It's more protected here and we can keep an eye on it.'

Bryn heaved an exaggerated sigh. 'Oh, God, he thinks he's Robinson Crusoe now! Can't it wait? We've only just sat down.'

'It would be safer to do it now,' said Josh. 'I know we're all tired, but if the boat breaks loose we're going to be stuck here and it might be some time before anyone finds us and we really will get a chance to play Robinson Crusoe. It's just a question of walking it round the shoreline. I could do with a hand, though.'

'Take Elvis,' said Bryn dismissively. 'The boat is his responsibility.'

'Elvis is barely more than a child.' Josh glanced at where the boy sat slightly apart, not listening to what was going on but with his head slumped onto his knees. 'He's exhausted.'

'We're all exhausted! For God's sake—'

'Why don't we rest for a bit?' suggested Aisling quickly as it became obvious that Bryn was working himself up for a rant. 'Then we can deal with the boat.'

Josh hesitated. Bella could see that he was really concerned about the boat, and somehow she managed to haul herself to her feet.

'I'll go with you,' she said, although her limbs felt like lead and she wasn't sure she could even get back to the other side of the island, let alone struggle through the water with a boat.

The wind whipped her wet hair around her face as she stood there, utterly bedraggled and swaying with exhaustion. Josh had an incongruous vision of her as she had looked at Kate's wedding, glossy in her hat and her high heels. He had always given her a hard time for being a bit of a princess, but there was no doubt about it: she was a princess with guts!

Her offer shamed a couple of the other men into going with them and, although Bryn resolutely maintained that the expedition could wait until they had all recovered, the four of them set off straight away. They were only just in time, too, as the boat was straining at its makeshift mooring and it wouldn't have been long before it dragged itself free and smashed into the rocks.

Bella had expected it to be hard work to move it round to the other side of the island, and in the event it was much more difficult than even she had imagined. There were times during that terrible trip when she was sure they would never make it.

For most of the way, the water wasn't too deep, but the boat was difficult to manoeuvre in the choppy sea. The rain blinded them, and the waves pounded relentlessly at them, knocking them off their feet and pushing them back towards the rocks.

At a couple of points they had to edge their way carefully around rocky promontories, where the footholds were slippery and uneven, and the water deeper. Bella slipped and was submerged several times, and once she disappeared completely under the boat before Josh thrashed frantically through the water to drag her back, gasping and choking, to the surface.

He kept them all going by sheer will-power, shouting

encouragement and refusing to let them give up. Bella's hands were numb, but just when she was sure that she couldn't hold onto the boat a moment longer, the beach came in sight. The others were there to help pull it up to safety, but by then Bella couldn't even make it to the cover. She collapsed onto the sand, heedless of the thrashing rain, unable to move a second more.

The next moment she found herself lifted in strong arms as Josh carried her the last few yards. 'I'm all right,' she roused herself to protest, knowing that he must be as exhausted as everyone else. 'Put me down before you fall down!'

'Stop wriggling and shut up,' said Josh, raising his voice above the sound of the wind.

'Well, that's not very lover-like!' Bella pretended to be offended. 'We *are* supposed to be engaged, you know.'

She had wanted to make Josh smile, but although the corner of his mouth quirked upwards, his eyes were deadly serious as he laid her down under the awning.

'I hadn't forgotten,' he said.

Bella was embarrassed to find herself greeted as a heroine by the women who had stayed behind. In the way women do, they had contrived to make the makeshift shelter as much of a home as they could, ranging the bags around the edge, laying out towels and sarongs as sleeping mats, and setting out the iceboxes as a table. Bella half expected to see that someone had hacked their way into the undergrowth to find some flowers.

It was Cassandra who noticed that Bella's foot was bleeding and promptly whipped the towel out from beneath her leg. 'That's a really bad cut,' she said with a grimace.

'I must have done it when I slipped on the rocks. Those sandals were designed for walking to and from the pool, not clambering over rocks.' Bella contemplated her ruined shoes sadly. They had been her favourites, delicate, strappy affairs with appliquéd flowers and sequins. 'They're never going to be the same again!'

'You should be worrying about your foot, not your shoes,' said Josh sternly, lifting her left foot to inspect the unpleasantly jagged tear along one side. 'Cassandra is right. That's really nasty. Why didn't you say something?'

'I didn't know I'd done it. I still can't feel it, to tell you the truth.'

She could feel his fingers gently probing around the cut, though. He must be as cold and as wet and as numb as she was, but his hands were wonderfully warm against her skin.

Bella studied her foot with an odd air of detachment. She was usually a terrible baby about anything like that, and if she'd cut herself in London would have been squealing and yelping and demanding emergency treatment, preferably from a tall, dark, good-looking doctor in a white coat who might or might not have an uncanny resemblance to George Clooney. *E.R.* just hadn't been the same since he had left.

It was strange to be thinking about *E.R.* when she was stuck on an uninhabited island in the middle of the Indian Ocean with the wind howling and screaming and shaking the awning, and the rain thundering down onto their pitiful shelter, and Josh and Cassandra peering at her foot in concern.

'Must it be amputation, doctor?' she asked solemnly, and Josh's smile did more to warm her than a lorry load of duvets and hot-water bottles.

Although Bella wouldn't have said no to a nice, warm, dry bed right then. With Josh in it.

'I think you'll survive,' he said, breaking into her fantasy. 'You're going to need some stitches, I think, but we'll just have to tie it up for now.'

After a fruitless search for something that could be used as a bandage, Josh tore a wide strip off the bottom of his short-sleeved shirt. Like Bella's foot, it had been thoroughly soaked in sea water so at least had the advantage of being cleaner than any of the alternatives.

He bound up her foot with a brisk professionalism. 'There, how does that feel?' he asked as he secured it with a knot.

'Better than a pedicure,' said Bella.

Wet and weary as she was, she felt bizarrely happy. The storm was no longer terrifying, but merely background noise to the fact that she was with Josh and that horrible tension between them had been blown away along with their plans for a peaceful afternoon snorkelling.

Later, they shared out the food from one of the iceboxes. Bella was almost too tired to bother by then, but Josh told her roughly that she had to eat, so she chewed obediently on a sandwich. Packed into plastic boxes and sealed in the icebox, the food had stayed miraculously dry, and once they had started eating they all discovered that they were ravenously hungry. Eyes began turning to the other two iceboxes.

'Do you think we should keep the rest for later?' Cassandra asked, turning instinctively to Josh as their unelected leader.

'I think it would be a good idea,' he said. 'We should put out the empty icebox, too, and collect some rainwater.'

Bryn rolled his eyes to the awning above their heads where the rain was already gathering in another great pool. They had to keep knocking the canvas to send it cascading down the sides to stop the awning collapsing beneath the weight of the water.

'I wouldn't have said shortage of water was our problem here!' he said sarcastically.

'It might be when the storm passes,' said Josh evenly. 'I didn't see any fresh water on the island and it's best to be prepared. The boat got pretty bashed around on those rocks. If we can't get the engine going tomorrow we might be here some time and in that case the one thing we're going to need is water.'

'I'm sure you'd love that,' sneered Bryn. 'It would give you a chance to show off all those survival skills of yours. I can just see you rubbing sticks together to make a fire and impressing the girls by spearing a fish!'

'It wouldn't just impress the girls,' said one of the men who had helped bring the boat round. 'It would impress me too!'

'Yes, shut up, Bryn!' said Aisling sharply, getting up to put the empty icebox outside to catch the rain. 'You're behaving like a spoilt child!'

'Oh, right, just because I don't jump whenever your precious Josh says jump! Who put him in charge anyway?'

'He's in charge because he knows what he's talking about, which is more than I can say for you!' Aisling snapped back.

'If he's so perfect, why didn't you stick with him?' snarled Bryn.

'I'm beginning to wish I had!'

'Oh, well, fine!' he said petulantly. 'Just because I'm not macho man like Mr SAS over there!'

'You can say that again,' murmured Cassandra in Bella's ear. 'Did you know that his name is really Bryan? I had to collect in all the passports, so I queried it when the names didn't match. Apparently he dropped ''a'' because he thinks Bryn is sexier and suits him better. Talk about self-deluded!'

Bella was delighted to have her theory confirmed, but hoped that Cassandra hadn't picked up on Bryn's jibe about Aisling leaving Josh.

She had, of course. Bella knew that she would have pricked up her ears at that too, and she was beginning to feel that Cassandra might be a kindred spirit.

'What was that about Aisling and Josh?' she asked curiously. 'Did they use to go out?'

'They were engaged briefly,' admitted Bella reluctantly, and Cassandra shot her a perceptive glance.

'No wonder you didn't like it when they went off diving together all the time! You don't need to worry, though,' she went on comfortably. 'It's obvious that he absolutely adores you.'

Bella knew that Josh adored her, but not in the way Cassandra meant. Until she realised how much she loved him, she would have said the same. 'Oh, yes, I adore Josh,' she would say if anyone commented on how nice he was, or how close they seemed, but she had meant as a friend, not as a lover.

Not the way she wanted him to adore her now.

Josh had ignored Bryn's taunts, and had gone out to check on the boat, leaving Bryn and Aisling to argue in snappy whispers. When he came back, he lay down beside Bella and, without a word, lifted an arm so that she could nestle into him, too tired to worry about looking clingy or needy or revealing too much and needing only the warmth and comfort of his body.

'How long do you think those sandwiches will last?' she asked sleepily. Lying close like this, they could talk without being heard by the others above the sound of the rain and in the darkness it was like being in their own private world.

'They'll stretch to breakfast,' said Josh. 'I wouldn't bank on any lunch if we can't get the boat going.'

'I hope we don't have to revert to cannibalism,' she murmured. 'We might end up like that parlour game where you have to argue that you're so essential that you shouldn't be eaten, and I'd be bound to be the first one in the pot. It's true,' she said as she felt Josh shake with quiet laughter. 'I must be the most useless person here. PR isn't exactly a survival skill!'

'Making people laugh is,' said Josh. 'You're a lot more useful than most people here, but if it comes to it, I'll make sure you don't get the short straw.'

'Thank you.' Bella snuggled into a more comfortable position with her arm across his chest. 'Anyway, I get the feeling that awarding the honour of first in the pot to Bryn would be a popular move!'

Josh laughed softly. 'He's just scared like rest of us.'

'*You* weren't scared,' said Bella.

'Yes, I was.'

Josh thought about how terrified he had been when she had slipped out of his sight under the waves and wished he could tell her how essential she was to him. Unable to resist the temptation, he put his other arm around her and held her close into him. They might not be very dry or very warm or very comfortable, but at least she was here and she was safe.

The storm passed as suddenly as it had hit them. One minute the darkness was filled with the sound of the savage wind and lashing rain and the next there was a silence so deafening that for a moment none of those awake could actually believe that the awesome noise had stopped. There was just the slow drip, drip of the palm leaves and the trickle of left-over water running off the awning.

Bella heard it stop too, and felt guilty for being the only one to experience a pang of regret. The storm had at least given her a chance to lie in Josh's arms. Now that it was over, there was no excuse not to go back to reality, to being careful, to remembering that they were friends, not lovers.

It was too dark to do anything about the fact that the storm had passed, so one by one they all drifted off to sleep again. Bella was horribly stiff when she woke the next morning, and her foot throbbed painfully. She told herself that it must be a good sign that she could feel it now, but couldn't help wishing that it would go back to being numb. She felt awful, damp and dirty in a way she had been too tired to feel the night before.

Limping outside, she found most of the party grouped anxiously around the boat. Josh and Elvis were peering into the depths of the engine and there seemed to be a lot of tinkering going on.

'They can't start the engine,' Cassandra whispered to Bella. 'Just as well we didn't eat all those sandwiches. Do you think Josh really knows how to spear a fish?' she asked hopefully.

'I'm not sure about that. He's usually quite good on engines, though.'

The words were barely out of Bella's mouth before a cheer went up as the engine spluttered into life and Josh looked up with a grin that told Bella just how worried he had been.

'OK!' he said, clapping Elvis on the back. 'Let's finish off those sandwiches and then let's go!'

Although the centre of the storm had moved on, it had left behind a sullen sea and dreary blanket of grey clouds that eked a constant drizzle that was almost more depressing than the rain had been. It wasn't cold, but everyone was tired and sick of being wet, and very nervous in case the boat broke down again, so after the first euphoria of leaving the island, it was a silent journey.

Aisling and Bryn were pointedly not talking to each other, and the atmosphere was so oppressive that the sight of the rescue boat at last came as even more of a relief than anyone had anticipated. They were still a couple of hours from the jetty, and transferred eagerly onto the faster boat, except Josh, who volunteered to stay on the boat with Elvis to talk to the authorities and make sure he didn't get blamed.

'We'll follow you in,' he said.

As the rescue boat sped away, Bella looked back at him, sitting calmly beside the boy in the tattered remains of his shirt and her heart turned over with love for him.

With its powerful engine, it was no time at all before the rescue boat had them back at the hotel, receiving the exclamations and commiserations of the others. The hotel looked as if it had received a fair battering from the storm itself, but a single night sleeping on the wet sand had been enough to make the rooms seem so luxurious as to feel faintly surreal.

A doctor, not looking remotely like George Clooney and not even wearing a white coat, was summoned to stitch up Bella's foot and give her a jab. The foot was swollen and very painful by then, and Bella couldn't help wishing like a baby that Josh was with her to hold her hand. Really, she had to stop being so pathetic!

At least she had had a shower, and not just any shower. Indisputably the best shower of her life. Bella washed her hair three times to get rid of the salt and the sand and, when at last she felt clean and dry, she lay on the bed to wait for Josh.

It had started to rain heavily again by the time Josh

finally appeared. There was no wind this time, and Bella could see the rain falling in a steady downpour beyond the veranda and hear it drumming loudly on the roof above her head. She had been dozing, and the room was so dark that she switched on the bedside lamp to squint at her watch, amazed to see that it was late afternoon still and there was a good hour until dusk.

The sound of Josh's key in the door, made her struggle up onto the pillows and stretch luxuriously. 'You've been ages,' she said. 'Is everything OK?'

'They wanted to give Elvis a hard time for taking the boat out at all, poor kid,' said Josh, sitting down on the edge of her bed. 'I think I persuaded them that it wasn't his fault.'

She had been waiting and waiting for him to come, and now he was there, sitting solid and safe beside her, and she felt suddenly shy again. 'What happened to your shirt?' she asked, to stop herself flinging her arms around him and burrowing into his strong, sure body.

'I think they felt it was rather indecent, so someone gave me this one when they let us have a shower.' He plucked at the shirt, a luridly coloured affair with a florid pattern. 'Do you like it?'

'To be honest, I wouldn't have said that it was quite *you*.'

Josh's smile gleamed in the dim light and their eyes met and held for a moment before they both looked away.

It couldn't be said that there was a silence with the rain crashing down on the roof, but there was a funny, breathless little pause that set Bella's heart slamming slowly and painfully against her ribs. At least Josh wouldn't be able to hear it with the racket the rain was making.

'How's the foot?' he asked after a moment.

'Sore.' Bella lifted her foot slightly to show him. 'They

stitched me up and gave me a new bandage. I don't think they thought much of your other shirt either.'

Josh took her foot and held it gently in his hand. 'I shouldn't have let you help move the boat around,' he said. 'I should have insisted one of the other men came with me and to hell with what Bryn thought. It was too dangerous for you to be out there.'

'If it was too dangerous for me, it was too dangerous for you,' she pointed out. 'Anyway, I only cut my foot. It's not as if I was bitten by a shark or got swept out to sea.'

'You could have drowned,' said Josh, refusing to be comforted. 'Last night you said that I wasn't scared, but I was. When I saw you slip and disappear under that boat, I was absolutely terrified.'

His hand had moved almost absently up to Bella's ankle. She swallowed. 'I knew you'd save me.'

She hesitated, torn between giving in to the sheer tantalising pleasure of his hand smoothing up her leg and the need to tell him how she felt. 'You saved all of us,' she said. 'I don't know if we would have survived without you. I was so proud of you, Josh. The rest of us went to pieces at the first hint of danger, but you knew exactly what to do.'

She smiled waveringly. 'I understand why people go off on expeditions with you now.'

Josh's hand had reached her knee. 'I'd have you as my second-in-command any day,' he said.

'But I was useless! I didn't know what to do.'

'Yes, you did. You knew instinctively that when things get difficult you need someone who can defuse the tension, someone who can make people laugh in spite of everything, someone who can get on with everybody. Someone like you, in fact.' His hand was warm against her flesh. 'I was thinking that I should really take you on expedition one day. Do you think you'd like that?'

'That depends on whether I could take my hair-dryer or not,' said Bella a little breathlessly. She was excruciatingly aware of the touch of his hand on her skin, but it was hard to tell whether Josh even realised what he was doing.

'You could take it,' he allowed. 'Whether you would find anywhere to plug it in is another matter.'

Any further and his hand would be under her skirt. 'I think I'd have to take it as a matter of principle.' Bella was striving desperately to keep the conversation light, but she was having a lot of trouble breathing. 'And my best shoes, of course.'

'I'm afraid as expedition leader I'd have to draw the line at your shoes,' said Josh with mock solemnity. 'All high heels would have to be left behind. I'd need to maintain some kind of authority over my team.'

'Does that mean I'd have to call you "sir"?'

'Only in private.'

Unable to keep a straight face any longer, they both started to laugh, but the moment they made the mistake of looking at each other, their laughter died abruptly.

'I couldn't bear it when I thought I might lose you,' said Josh in a low voice. 'You're my best friend.'

'And you're mine.'

'Bella—' He stopped, his hand tightening against her leg as the air shortened between them.

'Yes?' Bella's heart was beating so hard that she could hardly breathe.

Josh couldn't put what he wanted to say into words. He just knew what he wanted to do. Very slowly, he leant towards her, giving her the chance to push him away, to make a joke, and break the moment which had them both in its spell.

But she didn't. She just sat there, her eyes dark with a desire that drew him irresistibly closer

He stopped a fraction of a breath away from her mouth, conscious that this was the moment of no return. They looked deep into each other's eyes, and in the end it was Bella who closed the gap, touching her lips with his.

It wasn't too late. One part of Josh's mind was very clear about that. He could draw back and leave it at a brief kiss that they could both pretend had only ever been friendly. He even knew that was what he should do.

But he didn't want to. Her response had been so piercingly sweet that he couldn't bring himself to stop, not now.

So he kissed her, the way he had been wanting to kiss her for so long, and it was as if their lips belonged together. Bella's hands slid up his shoulders to wind around his neck, and she was kissing him back, giving kiss for kiss as they sank down together on the bed.

Lost in the heady scent of her, Josh tangled his fingers luxuriously in her silky hair. He raised himself slightly to smooth the hair from her face, and his heart turned over as she smiled up at him.

'Best friends don't do this,' he said softly.

'Don't they?'

'Not normally.'

'This isn't a normal time,' said Bella, running her hands lovingly over his back. 'We survived a storm at sea, and now nothing seems normal. We can worry about what friends do when we know what normal is again.'

'It might be too late then,' warned Josh, but his touch belied the caution in his words, and Bella pulled him back down towards her.

'I know,' she murmured against his mouth, 'but let's not think about it now. Let's not think at all.'

*   *   *

Much later, as they lay softly together, Josh rubbed his hand tenderly up and down Bella's arm. He felt extraordinary. It had never been like that before, but mixed with the heart-swelling feeling of peace and absolute rightness was a tinge of regret.

They had been right to decide all those years ago that they would stick with being friends, because now it would never be the same again. From now on he would never be able to look at Bella and not remember this tropical afternoon, with the rain crashing on the roof and the rattle of the air-conditioner, and her warmth and her sweetness and the fire that had consumed them both.

How were they going to go back to being friends now? *This isn't a normal time*, she had said, and she was right. He mustn't assume that this meant more to Bella than the classic response to surviving a crisis. However much he might want it to happen, she wasn't going to have suddenly forgotten how she felt about Will. Josh told himself that he had to accept that and find some way of staying friends without her feeling awkward or embarrassed or having to pretend something she didn't feel.

Outside, the tropical night had fallen without either him or Bella noticing. The downpour had stopped abruptly at some point, too, and now the insects were resuming their chorus of rasping and whirring and clicking, punctuated only by the steady drip of rainwater from the veranda roof.

'It's just as well we don't get out of dangerous situations very often,' he said.

Pressed into his side, with her leg entangled with his and her arm over his chest, Bella was feeling utterly content, replete down to her fingertips and toes, and half-surprised to find that her body wasn't glowing with satisfaction in the dark.

She didn't want this moment to end, but Josh's wry

comment was bringing reality seeping back. It might feel
as if everything had changed, but nothing had really. In
theory, they were both free agents, but it might not feel
that way to Josh. There was Aisling to think about, and
although Bella knew there was nothing between her and
Will, that wasn't what she had told Josh.

Now was not the time to tell Josh that she loved him,
not Will. He would think that she was just saying it because that was the kind of thing women said when they
slept with you.

But perhaps she would be able to tell him when they
got home, Bella told herself hopefully. Surely he couldn't
have made love to her like that if he was still bound up in
Aisling? Bella could think of plenty of ex-boyfriends who
were more than capable of separating sex from emotion,
but she didn't think that Josh was like that.

On the other hand, he *was* a man, she remembered, confidence fading rapidly. She was so used to thinking of him
as a friend that it was easy to forget that.

No, she wasn't going to spoil this moment by going all
intense and emotional on him, Bella decided. Much better
to show him that she wasn't going to put any pressure on
him. Let him go home and return to normal. He needed to
decide for himself that Aisling wasn't what he wanted and
then perhaps she could tell him how she felt.

In the meantime, she would treat things lightly. 'Is this
how you always react after a crisis on expedition?' she
asked.

'I wouldn't say that,' said Josh dryly, 'but sex is a common human reaction to a disaster.'

'We weren't part of a disaster, though.'

'We were lucky,' he said soberly. 'Things were pretty
touch-and-go for a while yesterday.' His arm tightened
around her as he remembered how close he had come to

losing her. 'If we hadn't made the island when we did, I'm not sure how long we could have kept that boat afloat.'

He hesitated. 'Is this going to change things for us, Bella?'

'You mean being friends?'

'Yes. I don't want it to affect our friendship.'

'Nor do I,' said Bella, unable to resist the temptation of smoothing her hand over his chest in a way that a mere friend would never do. 'I don't think it has to, not if we don't let it. Like you say,' she went on, proud of her casual tone, 'we were both reacting to a crisis. It might be different for you, but that was the closest brush to danger I've ever had. It's been a strange experience, and it still doesn't feel quite real. And if it feels like that here, it's going to seem even more like a dream when we get home. Perhaps we should think about it like that.'

It *would* seem like a dream, Josh thought. 'You think we should pretend it never happened?'

Bella wasn't sure that she would be able to do that. 'I meant more that this is like time out of time,' she said, struggling to find the words to explain. 'The usual rules don't apply.'   .

From her comfortable position nestled against his shoulder, Bella couldn't see Josh's face, but she could practically feel him lifting an eyebrow. 'The usual rules?' he echoed. 'What are they?'

'That we're friends, good friends, and being friends is important for both of us, and it's not something we confuse with…with this.'

'With sex?'

'Exactly,' said Bella, who had begun to flounder. 'We're going home tomorrow anyway. Then it'll be back to reality, and we'll go back to being just friends, and tonight will just be something that happened, and was wonderful, but doesn't have any connection with the way we are at home.'

She lifted her head slightly to look at him anxiously. 'Does that make sense?'

'I think so,' said Josh. 'Everything will be different tomorrow.'

'It's not tomorrow yet,' said Bella, letting her fingers drift suggestively.

'That's true.' Josh shifted so that she lay beneath him, and kissed the curve of her shoulder. 'Are you thinking we should make the most of tonight while it still seems quite real?'

His hand traced her contours, lingering lovingly on the curve of her hip, and Bella arched with a shiver of pleasure as she felt him smile against her skin.

'I think perhaps we should,' she agreed breathlessly and wrapped her arms around him to pull him closer.

CHAPTER TEN

'ARE you hungry?'

'Starving,' said Bella, and as if to underline the point her stomach let out an embarrassingly loud gurgle.

Josh laughed and patted her tummy. 'It sounds like it. Shall I go and see if I can find something to eat?'

Bella stretched across him to peer at the illuminated alarm clock by the bed. 'We've missed dinner. Pity there's no room service here.'

'The kitchens will still be open,' said Josh, getting out of bed and searching on the floor for his trousers. 'Having survived a near shipwreck, I can't let you succumb to starvation.'

He was gone for what seemed like ages, but Bella knew that he wouldn't come back empty-handed. Josh was nothing if not resourceful. When he did finally appear, he was carrying a tray laden with freshly cooked fish and steaming vegetables, all steaming hot, as well as two ice-cold beers.

'How on earth did you organise all this?' asked Bella, impressed, as he laid the tray on the bed with a flourish.

'It turns out that Elvis is the nephew of the barman and one of the cooks,' Josh told her, wondering if she knew how desirable she looked with her hair all tousled and her skin glowing.

'He told them how I went with him to the police to tell his story, and now they're insisting on treating me like some kind of hero, although I didn't really do anything. It was quite embarrassing,' he said, remembering his reception in the kitchen with a grimace. 'And when I asked if there were any leftovers from dinner, I was made to have a drink at the bar while Elvis's uncle cooked all this from scratch.'

Bella sniffed appreciatively. 'It smells wonderful,' she said, settling herself more comfortably against the pillows. She smiled at Josh. 'You *are* a hero,' she said. 'Anyone who can arrange a meal like this at this time of night definitely gets to be a hero in my book!'

They ate everything, sitting up in bed and then lolling across it to pick at the last few bits, and chatting easily. It felt extraordinarily relaxed, Bella thought at one point. There should have been *some* constraint, surely, given what they had been doing earlier?

But no. It seemed quite natural to be lying here with Josh, aglow with remembered delight, her foot sliding up and down his calf, while they talked and laughed exactly the way they had always done before.

Afterwards they walked—or in Bella's case, hobbled— down to the beach, where they sat in the dark shadows underneath the leaning palms and listened to the soft shush of the waves against the sand. The rain clouds had mostly dispersed by now, and the moonlight cast a shimmering silver stripe across the water. Above their heads, the faintest of warm breezes rustled the palm leaves.

'It's so peaceful,' sighed Bella contently, leaning back against Josh.

'Hard to believe what it was like last night, isn't it?' said Josh.

He was trying not to think about how soon tomorrow would come. He couldn't stop touching her now, couldn't control the way his hands moved lovingly over her, couldn't bear to think that this might be the last time he could hold her like this.

'I feel as if I could sit here for ever and look at the sea

like this,' she was saying, but he could feel her quiver of response.

Make the most of it, wasn't that what they had agreed?

'Forget the view,' he murmured, and drew her down into the soft sand for a long, sweet kiss that was followed by another, and then another, until the sand began to get in the way.

'You'll never get the sand out of your hair,' he said contritely, twisting it between his fingers and feeling how gritty it was.

'Perhaps I should cut it off before I go on that expedition of yours,' said Bella lazily.

Josh hated the thought. 'You must never cut it,' he said, appalled. 'It's beautiful hair.'

'I thought you would approve of the idea. It would be so much more practical.'

'Maybe,' said Josh. 'But it wouldn't be you. I—' He caught himself just in time. 'I *like* you as you are,' he finished.

When they went back to the room, he made her sit on the veranda while he brushed all the sand out of her hair with long, loving strokes, and then they went back to bed and made love again with a kind of urgency, as if they both sensed that the night was short and that seconds were ticking away.

The airport the next morning was crowded and chaotic. It was only a small terminal and, judging by the cacophony of languages, there were several flights leaving for various parts of Europe all at the same time.

Josh dealt with the luggage while Bella waited to one side. She felt cut off from the bustle around her, as if she were still wrapped in the bubble of enchantment from the night before. They had moved quietly around the room as they got ready to leave, saying little. There was nothing they *could* say, thought Bella.

'How's your foot?'

Wrenched out of her bubble of enchantment, Bella turned to see Aisling looking tired and strained.

'It's fine, thanks,' she said. Aisling was the last person she wanted to talk to this morning, but she would have to be pleasant for Josh's sake. 'It looks worse than it is really,' she said, nodding down at the professional bandage. 'How are you?'

'Feeling as if I've made the most monumental mistake,' said Aisling frankly. 'Bryn and I had the most terrible row when we got back. That awful time on the boat and then on the island made me realise that he's not half the man Josh is. I've been so stupid,' she sighed. 'I thought I loved Bryn, but I can see now that it was just infatuation. He's got quite a powerful position with C.B.C., and I think I was carried away by his good looks and all those status symbols he has.'

She bit her lip. 'I'm not even sure that he loves me,' she confessed. 'He said that he did, and that he was going to divorce his wife, but I wonder if he'll ever do it. I'd have been better off sticking with Josh.'

'Josh deserves better than being a safe option for you,' said Bella coldly. 'He's not just there for you to fall back on when things go wrong.'

'I know,' said Aisling. 'And I know it's too late. I just want to tell Josh that I realise what a fool I've been—and you how lucky you are,' she added.

The last enchantment from the night before trickled away, leaving Bella cold and exposed to hard reality. Aisling wanted Josh back. And she, Bella, was going to have to let him make that choice.

Every fibre of her being strained against standing back

and letting Aisling have another chance. Bella wanted to push her away, to tell her to leave Josh alone, that he was hers and always had been. But if she did that, she would never know if Josh had lingering regrets.

More than anything else, she wanted to spend her life with him, but not if she would always be wondering if she was his second choice, a fall-back position for him, easy and comfortable but not *really* what he wanted. She had told Aisling that Josh deserved better than that, and she did too. Josh would have to decide if he wanted Aisling or if he wanted her, and the only way he could do that was if she gave Aisling the opportunity to let him know she had changed her mind.

So she gave Aisling a brittle smile. 'Josh and I are just friends,' she said in a cool voice. 'You know that. He told you himself that we were just pretending to be engaged for this trip.'

'Well, yes,' said Aisling hesitantly. 'But I wondered whether the two of you had…?' She trailed off delicately.

'No,' said Bella. 'We're friends, and we want to stay that way.'

'Oh.' Aisling began to look more hopeful. 'In that case, maybe I'll have a word with Josh later.'

'Whatever.' Bella even managed a careless shrug. 'It's nothing to do with me.'

In some ways the journey back seemed longer and more unendurable than being caught by the storm. At least then she hadn't had time to think. Bella almost wished herself back there, frantically baling to keep the boat afloat, when all she had had to worry about was whether they would sink or not, rather than wondering if she had just thrown away her own chance to be happy with Josh.

She was very tired. Neither of them had wanted to waste the night before sleeping, and she was afraid that if she fell asleep against Josh now, she would lose what little resolution she had.

The only way Bella could cope was by withdrawing completely, and Josh seemed happy to keep her at a distance. She longed to ask him whether he had spoken to Aisling and what he had said, but she knew that she mustn't. They were both being very careful not to talk about anything that might remind them of those long hours of sweetness.

Bella yearned to be back there in that moonlit room where time had been suspended for a while. Whenever she thought about the way they had kissed, the way they had touched, she couldn't believe that Josh didn't see as clearly as she did that they were meant to be together. But then she remembered what he had said about Aisling, and how they both agreed that their friendship meant more to them than anything. Being Josh's friend meant wanting him to be happy, and if he wanted Aisling, she would have to accept that being friends was enough.

It was late by the time they landed at Heathrow after a delayed connection in Paris, and Bella was so tired and her foot was so sore that she felt terrifyingly close to tears.

'Let's just get a taxi,' said Josh, retrieving her huge suitcase from the carousel and loading it onto the trolley with his own small bag.

'Sure. I can drop you off on the way,' she said, so that he knew that she wasn't banking on him coming home with her.

'Great,' he said flatly.

They nearly ran into Aisling as they turned to go through Customs. She was glaring after Bryn's departing back.

'He's just walked off and left me!' she said furiously. 'He's gone back to his wife in Dorking. Apparently she ''understands'' him in a way I'll never do—I bet she does!' she added venomously, and then her face crumpled. 'What am I going to do? I was staying with him in his London flat, but he hasn't even left me a key to go there tonight.'

'You'd better come with us,' said Bella. 'You can always stay with Josh—can't she, Josh? Most of your stuff must still be there anyway, isn't it?'

'That's true.' Aisling looked hopefully at Josh. 'Would you mind, Josh?'

What could he say? Bella seemed intent on pushing Aisling towards him. Presumably she was worried in case he forgot their agreement that everything would go back to normal now—as if it could! Josh thought bitterly. There was no normal any more as far as he was concerned.

He wanted to shout at her that he hadn't forgotten what they had agreed. How could he forget when she had spent the entire day making it very clear that last night was last night, and now was reality, and there was to be no muddling up the two? But she was obviously determined to make sure that he didn't misinterpret how sweet and loving she had been last night.

There was no need for her to make it quite so obvious that she was afraid that he would make a nuisance of himself. Josh felt raw, hurt by her mistrust but more by the realisation that Bella had meant what she said, and that the night they had shared wasn't going to be repeated.

Fine, he thought. He would leave her alone if that was what she wanted. 'Of course you can stay,' he said to Aisling, who was watching him anxiously. 'I didn't even get round to putting your stuff away. Let's go and find a taxi.'

'I'm sorry, Josh,' said Aisling as the taxi headed out of the airport through the tunnel. 'I think I might have blown our contract. Bryn was well on his way to convincing himself that the storm was all your fault, and he certainly won't forgive me for the things I said last night. I should have been more careful, but he made me so angry! And now I'm afraid that he'll veto any move to award us the contract now. He's got a lot of clout at C.B.C.'

'Don't worry about it yet,' said Josh. 'We'll just have to wait and see what they say.'

'I'll understand if you want me to leave the company now,' Aisling said miserably.

'Of course I don't want you to leave,' he said. 'You've been doing a great job. And you were right about going on this trip. I made a lot of other useful contacts this week, which I wouldn't have done if you hadn't encouraged me to go. Even if the major contract doesn't come through, I think it will have been worth it.'

Of course he didn't want Aisling to leave, thought Bella dully. Aisling could obviously do what she liked—dump him, humiliate him, jeopardise an important contract—and Josh would still want her to stay.

The taxi waited with its meter ticking outside Josh's flat while he and Aisling got out and unloaded their bags.

'Well…see you,' said Bella brightly.

'Yes.' Josh hesitated, as if he would have said more, but in the end he stepped back and closed the door. 'See you.'

As the taxi turned round, Bella watched him unlock the door to his flat and stand back to let Aisling go in first. He followed her in without even glancing back to where she sat all alone in the back of the taxi.

So that was that. The end of the holiday and back to reality with a vengeance.

The house was cold and empty when Bella let herself in. The taxi driver had taken pity on her and carried her case to the door, but with her bad foot it was a struggle even to get it inside on her own. She would have to unpack it at the bottom of the stairs as there was no way she would ever be able to carry it up to her bedroom.

Bella limped into the kitchen and put on as many lights as she could. She had always loved this house, but all at once it seemed sad and lonely, and much too big for one person. She wished Josh were with her. It wouldn't feel lonely then.

But Josh wasn't there. He was with Aisling. Bella slumped down at the table and put her head in her hands, torturing herself by imagining them together. Were they sitting on his battered blue sofa, happy just to be back together again? Perhaps Aisling was telling Josh how much she regretted going off with Bryn, and then Josh could pull her joyfully into his arms, telling her not to worry about it just as she wasn't to worry about losing them the contract. 'You've come back to me and that's all that matters,' he might be saying right now.

Bella buried her head in her arms and wept.

In spite of her tears, she was so tired that she fell straight into a deep sleep as soon as she dragged herself to bed. She woke late the next morning, feeling terrible. Her eyes were all puffy and piggy, and a nagging ache seemed to have taken up residence in the pit of her stomach. Bella identified it eventually as a feeling of sick despair.

And as if that wasn't bad enough, it was Monday morning and she had to go to work. Somehow she was going to have to get herself out of bed and pull herself together!

One look in the bathroom mirror was enough to convince her that she was going to have her work cut out. She looked almost as bad as she felt. Bella sighed.

She had to face Phoebe and Kate, too. They had insisted on coming round to hear about the trip that evening. 'And don't think you can get away with just telling us it was fine,' Phoebe's message had warned. 'We want to know *all* about it!'

At least her eyes had gone down a bit by then, and she still had some colour from her days on the beach which helped disguise what would otherwise be a horribly white and strained face. Considering the oppressive cloud of misery that had been clinging to her all day and the rawness in her heart, Bella thought she looked pretty good.

Not that she fooled Kate and Phoebe for a minute. 'Bella, lovey, what on earth's happened?' asked Kate after one look at her face. 'You look absolutely terrible!'

'I don't look that bad, do I?' Bella asked Phoebe as she hugged her.

'Yes,' said Phoebe uncompromisingly. She held Bella at arm's length. 'What's wrong?'

Bella forced a bright smile. 'Nothing, unless you count my injury.' She showed them her bandaged foot. 'I'm not going to be able to wear any of my favourite shoes for ages.'

'That is bad,' agreed Kate.

'Exactly. Is it any wonder I'm not looking myself?'

'Well, come on, then.' They sat around the table where they had sat so many times when all three of them had shared the house and looked at Bella expectantly. 'Tell us all about it.'

'I don't really know where to start,' she said feebly.

'Start with the important thing,' advised Phoebe. 'How's Josh?'

'He's... He's...' Bella's throat closed so tight that she couldn't get any further. To her horror, her mouth began to wobble, and although she put up a hand to cover it, she couldn't hide the tears that scalded her eyes.

Phoebe looked at Kate. 'V&Ts all round, I think.'

'Yes please,' Bella managed to gasp. Now that she had started to cry she couldn't stop.

'I'll go,' said Kate, pushing back her chair.

There was a corner shop at the end of the road, and she was back a few minutes later, clutching several bottles of tonic. 'I brought chocolate too,' she said. 'I thought we might need it.'

Phoebe made the drinks and put a glass in front of Bella, who had given in completely by this stage and was sobbing with her head on the table. 'Come on, Bella,' she said, patting her on the back. 'This isn't like you. Here, have a drink.'

Bella lifted a blotched and tear-stained face and gulped immediately. It was so strong that she nearly choked, but when she had recovered, she took another, smaller, sip.

Silently, Kate handed her a box of tissues. Bella took one and blew her nose hard. 'Sorry,' she muttered, scrubbing at her cheeks with the crumpled tissue.

'We've all done it,' said Kate. 'Right here at this table too, in my case.'

Bella managed a watery smile. 'I remember.'

'And I seem to remember snivelling a bit over Gib,' said Phoebe, 'so we know what it's like.' She pulled out a chair and sat down next to Bella. 'Now,' she said firmly. 'You'd better tell us all about it.'

'Well!' exclaimed Kate when Bella had stumbled to the end of the story. 'I don't know why you're worrying, Bella. Even if we didn't know him, it's obvious that you're the one Josh loves.'

'Then why has he gone off with Aisling?' Bella demanded tearfully. 'He hasn't even rung to see if I got back OK.'

'You know, you could ring him,' Phoebe suggested gently.

'I can't,' she wailed. 'He's probably still in bed with Aisling, and even if he isn't, I can't start hassling him for attention. I said we would go back to being friends, but I'm not even sure I can do that now.' She groped miserably for another tissue.

'Of course you'll still be friends,' said Kate. 'You can't just stop being friends when you've been as close as you and Josh for all those years.'

'But that's the thing,' wept Bella. 'I don't think I can be friends if he's with Aisling. I couldn't bear seeing him with anyone now. But if we're not friends, I won't see him at all, and I couldn't bear that either. I don't know what to do,' she sobbed. 'I just know that I miss him, I miss him, I *miss* him…' Her voice rose to a wail.

Phoebe put an arm round her shoulder and exchanged a glance with Kate, who immediately launched into positive mode.

'I don't see Josh getting back together with Aisling,' she said. 'They never seemed that convincing as a couple. I never got the feeling they belonged together the way you and Josh do.'

'Kate's right,' said Phoebe, picking up the baton of encouragement. 'You and Josh are meant to be together and I'll bet you anything Josh knows that as well as you do.'

'Then why hasn't he rung?'

'Perhaps he's having problems getting rid of Aisling. You were the one who told us you thought he needed to be clear that relationship was over, so he probably feels that he has to sort that out and then he'll be round here like a shot!'

But Josh didn't come round. He didn't come round, and he didn't ring. He didn't email. He didn't even send a text.

Bella spent four days checking the phone to see if she had missed a call, although that wasn't likely as she took her mobile everywhere. Of course, his phone might not be working, she reasoned desperately, but then he could use the phone at work, couldn't he? Ditto computers. What were the chances that his laptop *and* his entire company network would crash at the same time? There had even been time for him to write her a letter and put it in the post!

'Do you think he might be ill?' she asked Phoebe on Friday morning.

'No,' said Phoebe patiently. 'I think he's waiting to hear from you. From what you told me about the way you were on the flight home, I think he's probably sitting there thinking that you don't even want to be friends any more.'

'Or he's too happy with Aisling to even think about me,' said Bella glumly.

'Well, you won't know until you talk to him, will you? Don't be silly, Bella,' said Phoebe sternly. 'Just ring him!'

In the end, Bella sent an email which took her ages to compose. She didn't want him to think that she had been pining, but she had to see him. So she pretended that she had been terribly busy and apologised for not being in touch sooner. Since she knew perfectly well that Josh hadn't even tried to be in touch with her, he wasn't to know that her inbox hadn't been jammed with messages and her phone permanently engaged, was he?

'What about a drink sometime?' she finished in what she hoped was a suitably casual way that would give him no indication of the degree of her desperation. Surely that sounded just like someone whose only concern was to pick up their friendship exactly where it had been before they had spoilt everything by sleeping together?

As soon as she had sent it Bella agonised about whether she had put it the right way. Every five minutes she checked her inbox to see if Josh had replied yet, and when his name finally popped up in bold, her heart lurched hammering into her throat.

God, she was in a bad way, she thought. It ought to take more than the sight of his name to reduce her to this state, but her hand shook on the mouse as she clicked to open the message.

'Doing anything this evening?' it read.

'Nothing special,' Bella typed quickly in reply. Apart from loving you and needing you and wanting you. 'Why don't you come round? We can have a bottle of wine and a chat. It'll be like old times!'

There, that didn't sound too intense, did it?

Josh's reply came back a few minutes later. Bella clicked eagerly. Perhaps he would say how much he was looking forward to seeing her, how much he had missed her even? Anything to give her some indication of what he felt.

She should have known better.

'OK,' said the message.

Bella was a terrible rambler when she got going, but Josh had succinct emails down to a fine art. They were always restrained, polite and to the point. Like him, really.

She was absurdly nervous before he arrived that evening, and dithered about the house wondering what to wear, how to look, how to *be*. It had never been a problem when she wanted to impress a man before. Kate had always said that she should have a Ph.D. in flirting, but she couldn't imagine flirting with *Josh*. She couldn't make play with her eyelashes or cross her legs or smile seductively at him. He would just ask her why she was fidgeting.

The peal of the doorbell broke into her thoughts, and Bella's heart jerked wildly. She had to take several deep breaths before she could even open the door, and when she did all the air evaporated from her lungs all over again at the sight of him standing there.

'Hi.' Her voice came out as a squeak, and Josh looked faintly surprised. *Not* a good start. Bella coughed. 'Sorry, frog in my throat,' she mumbled. She stood back. 'Come in.'

He was looking exactly the same as ever, she thought with a mixture of joy and despair. Joy because the mere sight of him now was enough to make her senses tingle and send happiness rushing along her veins. Despair because she could see no sign that she had the same effect on him. There was no outward indication that Josh had missed her at all, or that this evening was any different from all the other evenings when he had dropped round to see her as a friend.

He *did* look a little tired, though, Bella thought, studying him covertly as she got out a bottle of wine, but there could be lots of reasons for that. He wasn't drawn and puffy-eyed from crying himself to sleep every night like her, that was for sure.

'Have you been busy?' she asked as she rummaged for a corkscrew.

'Chaotic.' Josh sat down on one of the shabby sofas at the end of the kitchen. 'C.B.C. contacted us the day after we got back. They gave us that contract.'

'Really?' Bella looked up from the corkscrew in surprise. 'In spite of Bryn?'

'It turns out that the man who really makes the decisions at C.B.C. was on that boat trip as well,' said Josh. 'He was the short guy who helped us move the boat round the island. Anyway, he seemed to think that we were what their organisation needed.'

'Josh, that's fantastic news!' Bella was genuinely pleased for him. He had only set up his company a couple

of years ago and she knew how much he needed a big
contract like the one they had just won from C.B.C. to
make it secure.

'He was very taken with you,' said Josh. 'He went on
and on about how charming you were. I suspect you might
have done more than the rest of us to get us the contract.'

'I'm sure that's not true.'

Bella poured the wine and carried the glasses over to
the sofa. Handing one to Josh, she sat cross-legged at the
other end of the sofa, where there was no danger of touching him, and leant forward to chink glasses.

'Thank you anyway,' he said.

There was a pause. For a man who had just secured his
company's future, Josh seemed ill at ease. 'So, how have
you been?' he asked after a moment.

'Fine. And you?'

'Yes, fine.'

Talk about stilted conversation, thought Bella despairingly. Anyone would think they were on a blind date.

'I wasn't sure if you would be coming on your own or
not,' she tried again brightly. 'Where's Aisling tonight?'

'Aisling?' echoed Josh, as if puzzled by the question.
'I've no idea.'

The icy claws that had been clamped around Bella's
heart since that awful taxi ride back from Heathrow eased
their grip for the first time. Cautiously, it was true, but
definitely eased it. 'So you're not…?'

'Not what?'

'Not together again?'

'No.' Josh sounded almost cross.

'I'm sorry,' she said, afraid that she had touched on a
sore point.

'Why?'

Bella was flustered by the direct question. 'Of course I'm sorry if you're unhappy.'

'I'm not unhappy,' snapped Josh, and drank his wine morosely. 'Not about Aisling, anyway,' he added as an afterthought.

It was so unlike him to snap that Bella wasn't quite sure how to react. She eyed him a little uncertainly. 'Well, if it's not Aisling,' she said cautiously, 'what is it that's making you unhappy?'

Josh hesitated.

'You can tell me, can't you?' Bella persevered. 'A problem shared is a problem halved and all that. That's what friends are for, isn't it?

'That's the trouble,' said Josh, putting down his glass with a sharp click. 'I don't think I can be friends with you any more.'

He said it so seriously that for a moment Bella could only stare at him. Surely he didn't mean it? 'You can't just stop being friends, Josh,' she said in a voice that wavered in spite of herself.

Josh looked bleakly back at her. 'I just think it would be easiest if I didn't see you any more.'

'But…*why*?'

'Because being friends isn't enough for me any more.' He dropped his head into his hands as if unable to look at her stricken face. 'I'm sorry, Bella,' he said. 'I just can't do it. The last thing I want to do is to hurt you but I don't think I can stand it any longer. We should never have slept together that night,' he went on, not stopping to see her reaction. 'It's ruined everything. I knew it would. I *knew* we wouldn't be able to go back to the way we were before, and we can't, or at least, I can't. It was OK when I could just think of you as a dear friend, and I'm going to miss you more than I can say, but I'm too in love with you to be friends now, and I don't know how I'm going to bear not seeing you.'

The words were pouring out of him in a rush. Bella had never heard the self-possessed Josh sound so incoherent, and it took her a few moments to realise what he had said. When she did, she swallowed hard.

'Josh—'

But it only came out as a whisper, and Josh was still talking. Now that he had started, he seemed unable to stop.

'I haven't known what to do,' he was saying in despair. 'I was desperate to see you, but I knew that if I did I would just want to kiss you, and it's no good. I know you want us to stay friends, but I can't. I can't do it, Bella.'

'Josh—' she tried again.

'I'm sorry, I'm sorry, I don't want to embarrass you.' He hadn't even heard her. 'God, this is awful, but I have to tell you I love you. I *love* you,' he said again despairingly. 'I don't think I can manage without you, but I know how you feel about Will, and I know nothing is ever going to be the same again and—'

'*Josh!*' Bella had to shout in the end, and he stopped as if she had slapped him in the face. 'Will you please shut up a minute and let me say something?' she asked him.

He looked cautious. 'Yes.'

'I am not in love with Will,' she said very clearly. 'I do not want him. I want you.'

It was Josh's turn to stare. He kept opening and closing his mouth as if he couldn't decide which statement astounded him most. 'What?' was all he managed eventually.

'I only said that I was in love with Will because *you* were engaged to Aisling,' she told him. 'I thought it would be awkward if you knew how much I loved you then and it just seemed easier to let you believe that I was miserable about Will, but I wasn't. I was miserable because of you.'

'Easier?'

'Well, I didn't know that you loved me, did I?' Bella pointed out, exasperated.

They faced each other almost irritably until Josh finally registered what she had said.

'You're in love with me?' he said in disbelief.

Bella sighed. 'I think I've probably always been in love with you, Josh. It just took me a long time to realise, and when I did, it was too late, or it seemed that way.'

Josh was still having trouble assimilating what she was telling him. 'You *love* me?'

'Yes,' said Bella, going for the simple approach, which was all he seemed capable of understanding. She felt as if a huge smile had started inside her and was spreading out to her fingers and her toes and the ends of her hair and finally her lips. 'Yes, I do.'

'Bella…' Josh was still staring at her, but suddenly it sank in and he started to laugh. 'Bella,' he said again as he reached across the sofa and pulled her onto his lap and kissed her. 'Do you know how many years I've waited to hear you say that? Fourteen!'

'You're not going to try and tell me that you were in love with me all that time!'

'Of course I was! I fell in love with you at first sight,' he told her. 'You know perfectly well that you were gorgeous and irresistible, and you still are,' he said, kissing her again, and Bella wound her arms around his neck and kissed him back.

'Why didn't you tell me?' she mumbled against his throat.

'I knew you would never look at me,' said Josh, his hands moving hungrily over her. 'You were way out of my league! So I opted for friendship. I told myself that it was better than nothing, and I got used to the fact that you were going to end up with someone else. I didn't like it when I thought you were serious about Will, but you seemed so keen, there didn't seem much I could do about it.

'I think that's why I turned to Aisling,' he said. 'I thought she might be like you but the trouble was, she *wasn't* you. I was so relieved when she broke off the engagement!

'And you,' he said, pulling her down into the cushions and kissing her, long, deep, desperate kisses, 'you were so sympathetic, which was the last thing I wanted. You kept going on about being a friend and all I wanted was you. That's why I spent so much time with Aisling,' he told her. 'It was the only way I could think of to keep my hands off you!'

Bella sighed happily. 'For two people who know each other as well as we do, we seem to have got into a right old muddle,' she said. Her arms tightened around him. 'Is there anything else that I should know to avoid any more misunderstandings?'

'Only that I love you,' said Josh seriously, taking her face between his hands and looking deep into her eyes. 'I love you and I need you, and I want to come home every night and know that you'll be there. What do you think, Bella? Can we be lovers as well as friends?'

'Yes,' said Bella, pulling his head down so that she could kiss him again. 'We can, and we always will be.'

'This is all very mysterious!' said Gib, when Bella opened the door. 'All Phoebe will tell me is that we've been summoned to dinner and no excuses will be accepted. What are you girls keeping from me?'

'I've told you everything I know,' protested Phoebe, standing beside him. 'Tell him, Bella.'

'It's true. She doesn't know any more than you do. It's a surprise for everyone.' Bella smiled radiantly. 'Come in,' she said. 'Kate and Finn are already here.'

'Thank goodness you're here!' exclaimed Kate, hugging first Phoebe and then Gib when they went into the kitchen. 'Finn and I are dying of curiosity, aren't we, Finn?'

'I'm beside myself,' he agreed, deadpan.

'Well, *I* am,' said Kate when they all laughed.

'Me too,' said Gib. 'So come on, Bella! Don't keep us in suspense any longer. What is this big surprise?'

Bella looked at Josh, who smiled and took her hand. 'Bella and I are getting married,' he announced.

There was a moment's silence, then the four others burst out laughing.

'Well, we knew *that*!'

'That's not a surprise!' objected Phoebe.

'I agree,' said Kate. 'We've known for *ages*. I told Finn weeks ago that you were finally getting your act together.'

'I thought at the very least you were going to tell us you were having a baby!' said Phoebe.

'Well, it was a surprise to us!' Bella was inclined to be offended, but Josh was laughing too.

'It's no good, Bella,' he said. 'That's what comes of having good friends. They know you better than you know yourself!'

'But we're very, very glad you've come to your senses at last,' said Phoebe, making amends as she hugged them both.

'And about time,' Kate added, doing a swap. 'We were beginning to wonder if you would ever get round to it!'

'I think this makes it a hat trick, doesn't it?' said Gib

when the champagne had been opened. 'Three mock engagements, three happy endings!'

Josh put his arm around Bella and kissed her. 'Three happy beginnings,' he said.

Modern Romance™
...seduction and
passion guaranteed

Tender Romance™
...love affairs that
last a lifetime

Medical Romance™
...medical drama
on the pulse

Historical Romance™
...rich, vivid and
passionate

Sensual Romance™
...sassy, sexy and
seductive

Blaze Romance™
...the temperature's
rising

27 new titles every month.

Live the emotion

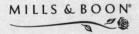

MB3

MILLS & BOON®

Live the emotion

Tender Romance™

OUTBACK BRIDEGROOM by Margaret Way

Christine is on her way back to Koomera Crossing – home to the only man she has ever loved...Mitch Claydon. Outback born and bred, Mitch is angry whenever he thinks of Christine. He'd loved her – even offered marriage – but she chose a life far away. And now, despite his best intentions, Mitch finds her as desirable as ever...

THE FORBIDDEN MARRIAGE by Rebecca Winters

When Michelle Howard finds herself agreeing to nurse Zak Sadler for the next month she's not sure what she's let herself in for. She is reluctant to get close to this sexy new Zak, whom she hasn't seen for two years – surely *any* relationship with him is strictly off-limits?

THE BOSS'S CONVENIENT PROPOSAL by Barbara McMahon

Ginny Morgan is desperately looking for the father of her child when she meets intriguing Mitch Holden. He's not the man she's looking for, but that doesn't stop him making a proposal. If she is willing to be his secretary, Mitch will pay for her son's operation...

THEIR ACCIDENTAL BABY by Hannah Bernard

When Laura discovers a break-in her gorgeous neighbour Justin Bane comes running to help her. But the intruder is a baby – left without explanation! As Laura and Justin are forced to learn the art of baby care – fast! – will Laura be able to stop herself giving her heart to both members of her unexpected family...?

On sale 3rd October 2003

Available at most branches of WHSmith, Tesco, Martins, Borders, Eason, Sainsbury's and all good paperback bookshops.

0903/02

1003/24/MB81

MILLS & BOON

The Pregnancy Surprise

Emma Darcy

Caroline Anderson

Gayle Wilson

When
passion
leads to
pregnancy!

On sale 3rd October 2003

*Available at most branches of WHSmith, Tesco, Martins, Borders,
Eason, Sainsbury's and all good paperback bookshops.*

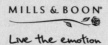

MILLS & BOON®

Live the emotion

PENNINGTON

BOOK FOUR

Available from 3rd October 2003

Available at most branches of WHSmith, Tesco, Martins, Borders,
Eason, Sainsbury's and most good paperback bookshops.

PENN/RTL/4

MILLS & BOON®

RAKES/RTL/2/8

Live the emotion

Another wonderful 6-book Regency collection

2 Glittering Romances in each volume

Volume 2 on sale from 3rd October 2003

Available at most branches of WHSmith, Tesco, Martins, Borders, Eason, Sainsbury's and all good paperback bookshops.

books | authors | online reads | magazine | membership

Visit millsandboon.co.uk and discover your one-stop shop for romance!

Find out everything you want to know about romance novels in one place. Read about and buy our novels online anytime you want.

* Choose and buy books from an extensive selection of Mills & Boon® titles.

* Enjoy top authors and *New York Times* best-selling authors – from Penny Jordan and Miranda Lee to Sandra Marton and Nicola Cornick!

* Take advantage of our amazing **FREE** book offers.

* In our Authors' area find titles currently available from all your favourite authors.

* Get hooked on one of our fabulous online reads, with new chapters updated weekly.

* Check out the fascinating articles in our magazine section.

Visit us online at
www.millsandboon.co.uk

…you'll want to come back again and again!!

WEB/MB

FREE

4 BOOKS
AND A SURPRISE GIFT!

We would like to take this opportunity to thank you for reading this Mills & Boon® book by offering you the chance to take FOUR more specially selected titles from the Tender Romance™ series absolutely FREE! We're also making this offer to introduce you to the benefits of the Reader Service™—

- ★ FREE home delivery
- ★ FREE monthly Newsletter
- ★ FREE gifts and competitions
- ★ Exclusive Reader Service discount
- ★ Books available before they're in the shops

Accepting these FREE books and gift places you under no obligation to buy; you may cancel at any time, even after receiving your free shipment. Simply complete your details below and return the entire page to the address below. **You don't even need a stamp!**

YES! Please send me 4 free Tender Romance books and a surprise gift. I understand that unless you hear from me, I will receive 6 superb new titles every month for just £2.60 each, postage and packing free. I am under no obligation to purchase any books and may cancel my subscription at any time. The free books and gift will be mine to keep in any case.

N3ZED

Ms/Mrs/Miss/Mr ....Initials ....
BLOCK CAPITALS PLEASE

Surname ....

Address ....

....

....Postcode ....

Send this whole page to:
UK: FREEPOST CN81, Croydon, CR9 3WZ
EIRE: PO Box 4546, Kilcock, County Kildare (stamp required)

Offer valid in UK and Eire only and not available to current Reader Service subscribers to this series. We reserve the right to refuse an application and applicants must be aged 18 years or over. Only one application per household. Terms and prices subject to change without notice. Offer expires 31st December 2003. As a result of this application, you may receive offers from Harlequin Mills & Boon and other carefully selected companies. If you would prefer not to share in this opportunity please write to The Data Manager at the address above.

Mills & Boon® is a registered trademark owned by Harlequin Mills & Boon Limited.
Tender Romance™ is being used as a trademark.